To Lydia

SHOR

and
a bit more

by

Piers Rowlandson

from

Piers

March 2023

Dedication

To my children and grandchildren.
A random collection for a rainy day.

CONTENTS

List of Characters

Stories 1-3
The Griffin Family, live in the Pink House, Cowes.
Father: Rick, born 1949 died 2021, Consultant ENT Surgeon. His first wife Annabel died of leukaemia not long after they married.
Mother: Sarah, (née Jones) born 1950 died 2013. Consultant Haematologist/Oncologist, was the oncologist who looked after Annabel.
Children:
Tori born 1988 married Paul Sampson parents of Ginny born 2011
Harry, born 1990. His partner is Judith.
Ben born 1992 married Angelica, parents of Amelia

The Sampson Family, live in the Manor House at Freshwater.
Father: Colonel John Sampson.
Mother: Clare.
Children:
Paul born 1986
Sally born 1988
Stable girl: Laura born 1980

The Saunders Family, live in the house across the river in Yarmouth.
Bob Saunders, sailmaker.
Children:
Angelica born 1988
Alec and Tony, distant cousins of the Saunders family (a few years older than Angelica).

Steve a sailmaker friend of Bob.

Giles, a rowing blue at Cambridge, briefly Angelica's boyfriend.

Baron Freddie von Braun owner of Zaca
Ursula his cousin
Captain Mike, Captain of Zaca.

Stories 4&5

Stevie: an undergraduate at Oxford.

Quentin: about fifteen years older than Stevie, a musician (saxophone player).

In New Zealand

Bob (not Saunders) is the owner of Blue Grass a Lidgard 38 (sailing yacht) He is about ten years older than Stevie.

Bob's crew: Tom 25, John 30, Dave 35 and Jake 40 years old (approximately).

Story 6

Denise and Martin are drama student at Chichester University.

Celia and Simon are apprentices at Rolls Royce.

1

Ben

"Hurry up Ben."

"I'm coming Dad."

It was a bright, clear morning with a light breeze from the south-west. Ben ran across the gravel and jumped into the Volvo. Rick drove over to Yarmouth Sailing Club.

"Are you sure you've got everything you need?"

"Yes, Dad, I'm not the one who forgets things."

In the boot of the car was Ben's sailing bag, stuffed full: a change of clothes, wet suit, life jacket, towel and sunblock. He was wearing dark glasses and his cap was on back to front.

"Where's your sister?" asked Angelica. For the last two summers Tori had sailed an Optimist dinghy in club races. Hers was almost new and finely tuned for racing. Ben had had to make do with an old plywood club boat. Tori and Angelica were the same age and fierce rivals.

"Riding," said Ben. "I'm sailing Sandpiper now."

"She's gone over to Freshwater Manor Farm. Ponies

are her thing now," Rick added.

Angelica pouted. "I don't believe you."

"It's true I'm afraid. You will have to put up with Ben. He's got Sandpiper now."

Optimists are small single hander dinghies for children under sixteen.

"You should have seen my Dad in the parents race last year, he could hardly wedge himself under the boom. His legs hung out over one the side and his head and shoulders the other. Once on-board he was stuck," said Ben.

"Never-the-less he managed to win the race, didn't he?" said Angelica. "I remember Tori whooping with delight."

Angelica was much taller and three years older than Ben. She looked down at him and smiled.

"I'll help you get rigged up then. It's going to be fun having a little brother."

"Thanks," said Ben. "I can manage."

"I'll help anyone who needs a hand," said Rick.

"Dad's just parking the car. He'll be along in a minute, but only to take my trolly. I've learnt the art of tuning Pickle and Dad doesn't interfere."

Bob walked up behind his daughter, he was laughing.

"I wouldn't dare!"

She spun round. "It's not fair creeping up on me like that."

Once the Oppies were rigged, the children hauled the boats across the grass and down the slipway. They sailed away towards the starting line.

Rick and Bob launched the club's patrol boat. They stationed themselves under the swing bridge that separated the river from the harbour. They were well placed to watch the start and also in a good position to prevent any inexperienced sailors getting swept under the low arch. The current was strong especially when the tide began to ebb.

Ben had only been sailing for two years; Angelica had five years' experience, so it was to Rick's surprise and delight that Ben crossed the line ahead of her, and kept going all the way to the bend in the river where they bore away into Mill Creek. However, tacking back out of the Creek, Angelica's greater experience and skill showed and she left the rest of the fleet standing. Ben had the common sense to watch what she was doing and follow in her wake. At the line she took the gun and Ben was fourth. She helped him pull his boat up the slipway and into the dinghy park.

"Well done, little brother," she said, grabbing his life jacket and swinging him round. They disappeared off in the direction of the changing rooms. Ben was flattered but also slightly annoyed by her teasing. He admired her and looked up to her as he looked up to his sister.

Throughout the summer Ben improved, but he never managed to beat Angelica.

"What am I doing wrong, Dad?"

"She's older, heavier and has sailed in the river longer than you."

"I think Pickle is faster. She spends ages polishing the bottom, and her sail is newer than mine."

"Well, you polish the bottom and I'll buy you a new sail."

Their efforts paid off and in light winds in the river Ben managed to win, occasionally. However, out in the Solent, especially on more windy days Angelica's extra wight and strength gave her the advantage and she easily won every race.

-§-

A year went by.

"It's the Lymington regatta, next week-end," said Bob.

It was another Sunday and the Saunders and Griffin families were sitting outside the club. Across the river was a large rather gloomy old manor house. It had been in Bob Saunders' family for generations.

"Is your house haunted?" asked Ben.

"No," said Angelica.

"Mum thinks our house is."

They had changed after sailing and were sitting on a bench close enough to overhear their parents conversation.

"Will you take the RIB over, like you did last year?" asked Rick.

"Why are they called RIBs?" asked Ben.

"Ridged Inflatable Boats," said Angelica. "Ridged because they have a fibreglass bottom and inflatable because of the enormous inflatable tubes that make up the rest of the boat, I thought everyone knew that, Ben."

"Well Angel, I bet you don't know what a martingale is."

"Yes I do."

"No you don't."

"It's a bird."

Ben shook his head and laughed. Angelica grabbed him and tried to tickle him. Ben struggled free and ran off. She pursued him, tackled him to the ground and sat on him. She went on tickling him.

"Stop it, stop it," gasped Ben.

"Say I surrender,"

"I… I surrender."

Angelica let him go. Ben darted off, shouting over his shoulder:

"I don't surrender."

The chase started all over again.

Rick watched them go and then turned back to Bob. They continued to plan the next week-end.

"Angelica's cousins, Alec and Tony, will be coming as well, so we will be towing four Oppies," said Bob.

"Sarah will bring the Volvo over so that we have transport to take us round to Uncle's house. I've arranged for us to stay there on Saturday night. I've got a set of keys"

"Excellent," said Bob. "I'm glad we don't have to arrange B&B."

"Alec and Tony will be moving on soon, won't they?"

"I should think so. Alec is really too large for an Oppie now. It's an advantage on really windy days but he can hardly squeeze under the boom."

"Whereas Angelica is the almost perfect weight and

build at the moment," said Rick.

Bob smiled. "Long may it last."

"It would be a pity if she stopped growing now," said Rick. "You wouldn't want her to be a midget."

"No," laughed Bob. "I'll have to bite the bullet and get her a Laser next year."

"Why not a 420? We could go halves and Ben could crew for her."

"That's an idea. I'll put it to her when the time comes."

-§-

Bob brought the RIB around to the pontoon by the club and Rick helped him tie each Optimist, one behind the other, onto the stern of the mother ship. The four children piled on-board and helped push off. Towing the dinghies through the harbour made quite a sight. A friend hailed them from one of the yachts moored up on the piles.

"You look like a mother duck leading her ducklings," he shouted.

"The wind speed is approaching 20kts in the gusts," said Bob.

"It may be too blustery to run a race," said Rick.

"The older ones will cope," replied Bob.

"I'm not sure Ben and the younger ones will," said Rick.

The conditions favoured Alec who was able to beat Angelica for the first time that season but Ben struggled to keep Sandpiper upright, sailing and bailing at the same time slowed him down.

"I'm exhausted," he complained when Rick and Bob came alongside in the RIB after the first race.

"Eat this and you'll feel much better," said Rick, handing him a Mars Bar.

"I hate Oppies. It's pointless trying to sail in these conditions. The boat takes on water all the time. Proper dinghies have self-bailers."

"Well Ben if you want to continue sailing; we'll have find you a more suitable boat."

In the next race Ben capsized. The younger and lighter children were all struggling. There were Oppies upside down all over the course. Patrol boats were dashing here and there, righting dinghies and taking them in tow. The few parents who had RIBs were gathering up their children and their children's friends.

"It's chaos," said Bob.

"I thought it might all turn to a bag of worms and it has," said Rick.

"It's difficult being Race Officer, but they should have cancelled the B fleet," said Bob.

"It can't be helped now," said Rick. "Let's concentrate on getting Ben and some of the others upright and ready for the tow back to the club."

Angelica and Alec had no such problems, they were battling it out for the lead. Sailing and bailing as they went upwind and then surfing down the waves on the next leg. Angelica had made a good start and was able to hang onto her advantage until the last beat when Alec got the better of her.

"Bad luck, Angel," shouted Bob.

"You'll get him next time," yelled Ben.

The RIB turned for home followed by the older sailors. A patrol boat brought up the rear.

"I think you've done really well, Ben. The conditions have been dreadful for Oppie sailing."

"Thanks, Dad."

Once the dinghies were put away in the Royal Lymington dinghy park, the children went off to shower and change. Rick and Bob waited for them on the decking outside the club. A high tea had been laid out.

Although they were only half way through the regatta there was a prize giving for the winners of the day. Alec got a glass for his triumph in the first race. Angelica got a pink rosette and a mug for being the first girl. Rick knew her well enough to tell from her body language that she was not happy. However, she managed a smile for the Commodore who was handing out the prizes.

"Well done Angel," Rick said as she walked back to their table.

Angelica bent to whisper in his ear. "I hate pink! I'm not that sort of girl."

Her father laughed. "A skull and crossbones flag would be more appropriate."

"No Dad! I'm not a little boy. I just want... want to be... Oh I don't know."

She did look very cross. Another girl's the mother overheard the conversation and turned round.

"You're quite right," she said. "The men who run this club are so old fashioned. Fancy giving a girl a pink rosette. Don't they know it's positively insulting."

"I love this club," said Ben. "The occasional eccentricity makes it all the more fun."

"Well said, very diplomatic," murmured Rick.

They laughed and the woman joined in. Ben looked confused.

"Why are you so cross, Angel?" he asked.

"Because I don't like pink."

"But you are a girl aren't you?"

That only made Bob and Rick laugh more.

Angelica picked Ben up in her arms and squeezed him so tight that he tuned blue.

"Yes, Ben, and as you are about to find out, the female is more deadly than the male."

"Quit fooling about and get your things out of the changing rooms," said Rick. "Mum will be here in a minute to take us all around to Uncle's place."

"I'm dying to meet your uncle," said Angelica.

"I'm sorry to disappoint you but he won't be there," said Ben.

"Oh, why not?"

"He spends nearly all his time in London, working."

"What does he do, up there in the smoke?"

"His company is based in the Strand and when he's not there he is attending to business in the House of Lords."

"I always wanted to meet a lord."

"He's just ordinary. He will be down for a few days in August."

"Is he a sailor?"

"Yes indeed. He used to do all the off-shore races, but now he's too busy."

They pushed out through the swing doors and found Sarah waiting for them in the car park.

"How did you get on, darling?"

"Oh Mum, don't ask. I was way behind Angel in the first race and capsized in the second."

"It was really too windy for most of the fleet," said Rick.

"They should have postponed. Conditions will be better tomorrow," said Bob.

"I really enjoyed it," said Angelica.

"So did I," said Alec. "And you still have a chance to get revenge tomorrow."

Angelica gave him a look.

"You're so right," she said.

Rick opened the boot and Angelica and Ben got into the two fold-down seats. Alec and Tony squeezed into the middle with Bob and Rick took the passenger seat beside Sarah.

"We need to get a people-carrier for these expeditions, some of the regattas will be near Birmingham." said Sarah.

Rick groaned, "I'm not keen on muddy puddles in the Midlands when we have the whole Solent on our doorstep."

"But if the children want to compete then we should at least give them the chance."

" OK, I'll look into it but I don't think we'll get much for this old bus."

They drove around to a large house overlooking the marshes and the Solent. In the distance was the Isle of

Wight and the line of the Downs stretching from the Needles to Newport. Rick let them into the hall. To the children's delight there was a suit of armour complete with visor, a mace dangled from his hand. There were crossed swords on the wall.

"Bring your things through to the extension," said Rick.

He lead them down a passage and into a part of the house that had been built on as lodgings for the crew in the days when his lordship had campaigned an ocean racer.

"Where am I going to sleep?" asked Angelica.

"In the girls' dorm. If I were you I'd sleep on the bottom bunk. It's surprising how often people fall off the top," said Rick.

"The other room is the boys' dorm. It has bunk beds for six so there will be plenty of room for the three of us," said Ben.

"Am I all on my own then?" said Angelica.

Sarah intervened. "Really Rick, you can't expect Angel to sleep down here. She can have the spare room and we'll have the room at the back of the house."

"Fair enough, and Angel can share our bathroom," said Rick "I'll start the supper."

They joined Bob in the kitchen. He was already cooking a huge fry-up. The others laid the table. Wine glasses for the adults and tumblers for the children.

"Will Angelica mind being separated from the boys?" asked Rick.

"Maybe. She likes to think of herself as one of the boys but that is beginning to change," Bob replied.

The meal was soon finished and the children went

through to the sitting room.

"An hour of television and no more, then bed," Sarah warned them.

The adults sat outside finishing off their wine while the sun went down over the New Forest.

-§-

Two years later Rick bought a 420 (French designed two person dinghy with spinnaker and trapeze).

"Angelica will love the new boat, don't you think, Ben?" said Rick.

"She said she's really excited."

"You two are about the same height and weight now so you could take it in turns to crew."

"I expect Angel will want to helm in the races."

"Whoever is best at tactics should crew," said Rick. "The helm has to concentrate on speed, making the boat go fast. The crew can be aware of what the rest of the fleet is doing and call the tacks."

"I know, Dad, but I also know Angel."

-§-

Tony and Alec had also bought a 420; the battle was on to see who could win the medium handicap trophy.

"Which of you is helming today?" asked Angelica.

"I am," said Alec.

"Then I'll ask Ben to let me helm," she replied.

Alec seemed to tower over her. He and Tony still had a weight advantage. Angelica gave him a look and smiled. He winked and turned away. Ben was turning out to be a cunning tactician. He seemed to be ahead of the others when it came to understanding tidal streams. They got afloat in good time and sailed slowly up and down the line, assessing the bias.

"We should take the pin end of the line and tack out into the last of the ebb tide, Angel."

The five minute gun went. Ben started his watch.

"Got it!"

"Count us down."

There was no need for Angelica to tell Ben, but she always did. He didn't mind, he accepted that she was in charge. He called out the minutes and then the final seconds. He was spot on and they crossed the line as the gun went.

Ben was out on the trapeze, keeping the boat flat, Angelica was watching the tell-tales and concentrating on speed. They were a fraction behind at first, but by tacking out into deep water, the stronger tide boosted their speed and they were soon well ahead of the boys who had started inshore. Ben called tacks. They were first around the windward mark and planed away towards the wing mark. Downwind they held their advantage but Alec and Tony began to catch up on the beat to the line.

"But not enough!" said Angelica, as they gathered in the clubhouse after the race. "You were still way behind."

She made a fist and pretended to punch Alec on the shoulder. He caught her arm and swung her around in a dance move so that they ended up entwined. Angelica stepped forward.

"Slow, slow, quick, quick slow!" she danced four or five steps forwards and Alec followed her.

"Come on Angel, let's queue up for lunch," said Ben and joined the others waiting by the hatch.

"I think Angel fancies Alec," said Tony.

"No, she doesn't," said Ben. "She thinks he's rubbish."

Tony laughed. "She's too old for you Ben."

Ben turned away and ordered bangers and mash and went to sit at a table by himself.

"Eating alone?" said Rick.

Ben didn't say anything.

"Have you fallen out with Angel?"

"No."

"Well you two have really got the hang of the 420. I think we should enter the Hayling Island regatta."

"Will Alec and Tony be going?"

"I'm sure they will. It's an international event."

The others joined them. Angelica sat down beside Ben and gave him a nudge.

"Were you so hungry, you couldn't wait for us?"

Ben smiled but said nothing. Alec was sitting on her other side and tried to claim her attention, Ben was secretly pleased that she turned her back on Alec and asked him to get her a pudding.

-§-

Getting two 420's, two adults and four children over to Hayling Island for the European Championships was a major logistical exercise. It involved borrowing the club's double trailer and loading it up the night before.

Rick attached it to the people-carrier and drove home. At crack of dawn Bob arrived with the boys and Angelica. They all piled into the big blue car and drove round to Fishbourne and, after a wait, onto the ferry. Rick queued up and ordered tea and toast, for them all. Angelica sat at a separate table and used a black permanent marker pen to stencil their sail number onto a new white spinnaker.

"Looks very neat," said Rick.

"Hope the measurer approves," said Bob.

"Why wouldn't he?" asked Angelica.

She moved over to the bench by the window and sat down between Alec and Ben; he's behaving as if he was her boyfriend, thought Ben. It gave him and odd, unfamiliar, confused feeling.

They drove round from Portsmouth to Hayling Island and unloaded the boats. In a shed the international measurer weighed and measured and inspected every aspect of each boat. He was not happy with the numbers on the spinnaker.

"Oh Dad, he said the 1 is too wide. What are we going to do now?" Angelica looked cross.

"I have some Tippex here," said Bob.

"It's like you have had this problem before," said Rick.

"I have indeed," said Bob and using a ruler to keep the edge of the number clean and straight, he narrowed the 1 to exactly the right width. Ben took the sail back to the shed and got it approved.

"Phew," said Angelica. "I didn't know anyone could be so picky. He even queried the weight of our compass, said it added weight to the boat. He implied that we had bolted it in place in order to make the boat seem heavier than it really is."

"Well thank goodness he relented on that one. Our boat is certainly not underweight." said Rick.

It was a big fleet with over a hundred dinghies on the water. The French team were the ones to beat but there were representatives from Ireland, Wales, Scotland and most of Europe. Rick made sure both boats were well provisioned with food and water.

"Scotch eggs were a good idea, Rick." said Bob.

"Less messy and more appetising than soggy sandwiches."

Bob and Rick watched from the shore. They had decided not to bring the RIB over.

With Angel at the helm and Ben on the trapeze, they manage to be in the top twenty all the time and in the top ten most of the time; their best was fourth. Alec and Tony were way down the fleet. It seemed Ben's tactical instincts were paying off. They were getting noticed even if they were not yet in the chocolates, as the saying goes.

For Bob and Rick it was frustrating: the racing was too far out to sea for them to be able to follow the action, even with binoculars. They thought a white spinnaker might stand out among all the coloured ones but it turned out that there were plenty of white ones. At that distance it was hard to distinguish the different coloured life-jackets.

"I'm sure that's Angel and Ben," said Bob.

A white spinnaker flashed out as the fleet started to round the bottom mark.

"But there's another identical one!" said Rick and laughed. "Let's go and get a drink. They won't be in for ages yet."

-§-

The last day of the regatta finished with prize giving followed by a disco. Tables and chairs were pushed against the walls and a DJ arrived with all the usual equipment, including flashing lights. Bob and Rick retired to the pub up the road.

Ben bought Angelica a soft drink and was mortified when she accepted a beer from Alec, now old enough to buy alcohol legally. All four of them put their drinks down on a table and started to dance. It was a kind of free for all at first but Ben found himself more and more on the edge of the floor while Alec and Angelica squeezed their way into the middle.

"Want a proper drink?"

Ben turned round to see Tony leaning towards him, shouting to make himself heard above the music.

"Yes," he nodded and they pushed over towards the bar. While Tony was waiting to be served, a girl slipped in beside him.

"How did you get on?" she asked.

"Oh we were rubbish. I think we were 46th overall. Our best result was 20th."

"You did better than us, then," she shouted in his ear.

Tony ordered two pints of Doom Bar and a glass of wine for the girl. The three of them sat down at a table. The new girl, who turned out to be called Barbara (or Babs for short) and Tony had to lean so close to each other to keep the conversation going that they their heads were practically touching. Ben, unable join in, got up and slipped out of the building. It was a warm night. The moon cast a luminous path across the estuary. He strolled along the beach, listening to the melancholy withdrawing roar of waves upon the shingle. He found the noise soothing to his jangled nerves. That was until he realised he was not alone. A few yards away a couple were lying on the sand, their arms around each other. They were kissing. It didn't take him even a second to recognise Alec and Angelica. He turned and walked away. He thought he had come to terms with the fact that Alec fancied Angelica. But he hadn't considered the possibility that she might be looking for a boyfriend. She was his special friend; he had taken that for granted. In the beginning he had looked up to her and Tori as if they were both his sisters. Since then Angelica and he had become close. Over the last five years they had spent so much time on the water together. Now he had an odd sense that he was losing Angelica and it hurt. It made him feel uncomfortable and confused. He screwed up his eyes and fought off the temptation to cry.

He went back into the club and sat down at the table, hoping Tony would buy him a drink. The DJ had started a slow number. Tony and Babs were swaying along in a tight embrace, and just as Ben spotted them, they started kissing. Everyone's at it except me, he thought and went out into the car park to await the return of Rick and Bob. He didn't have to wait long.

"Taking a breath of air?" Rick asked.

Ben nodded.

"Where are the others?" asked Bob.

Ben gestured towards the club, "Still dancing I expect."

Bob rounded up the older three and they all set off for B&B in a large house just up the road.

-§-

The major events were over for the year but there was still plenty of club racing going on. Angelica and Ben settled back into their Sunday routine: racing followed by lunch in the club with its views of the Solent and to Ben, the satisfying sight of the slow boats still struggling to finish.

"Are you missing Alec and Tony?" Rick set his plate and his drink on their table and sat down.

"Yes," said Angelica. "Without them we don't have much competition."

"I think Dad's asking if you're missing your boyfriend," Ben giggled and got kicked under the table for his trouble.

She smiled at Rick.

"He's not my boyfriend," she hissed in Ben's ear.

"He's gone up to Oxford, hasn't he?" Rick asked her.

"Yes. He's the brainy one in that family."

"He's reading Maths isn't he?"

"And physics."

"And so musical. I've a lot of time for Alec," said Rick.

Angelica looked as if she might be going to cry.

"Dad, don't be so insensitive. Can't you see she doesn't want to talk about him?" said Ben, and then to

Angelica. "Come on Angel, let's go and put the cover on the boat.

They left the building by the stairs that led down to the dinghy park.

"I'll never see him again," she said.

"Why not, Angel? He'll be down at Christmas."

"I don't want to see him again. I asked him to keep in touch and he hasn't: not one text, nothing. I did text him to see how he was getting on. But nothing, not one jot, not one tiny squeak."

Now she was crying. Ben patted her shoulder, and tried to put an arm around her. He had never seen Angelica cry. He never seen Tori or his mother cry for that matter and it made him feel anxious and unsure what to do.

Angelica wiped her eyes, blew her nose, threw back her head and laughed. "He's rubbish and I'm going to forget him. I'm too busy to even think about him. I've got to concentrate on getting to Cambridge."

Ben felt a lot better. It seemed that the old Angelica was back in control. He gave her a hearty pat on the back as if they had won a race or something. She caught hold off his sweater and swung him round.

"Come on, little brother, we've got things to do, people to see, places to go."

-§-

Angelica did get to Cambridge. Even though she had said that she would continue sailing with him in the 420, Ben knew that she wouldn't.

"It's not her fault, it's just that she's so busy these

days," he said.

"Yes, once you leave home, it's hard to keep up things like sailing or riding, as Tori is finding out," said Rick.

"The thing is it's so hard to find a crew. There's nobody who can replace Angel."

"Well I think we should sell the 420 and get you a Laser," said Rick.

-§-

Time flies by and it's Ben's first year up at Oxford, following in his sister's footsteps. History was his passion, particularly the Middle Ages.

"Wouldn't modern history be more interesting?" asked his father.

"Possibly, but you have to start somewhere and the coronation of Charlemagne in the year 1000 seems as good as any."

"Do you see anything of Tori?" asked his mother.

"Not much, she is so busy with her work and she has her own friends."

"Have you met Mike?"

"No, Mum, I saw them once on the river, hiding under a weeping willow tree. They thought they couldn't be seen, but I recognised Tori's voice and I'm sure Mike was in the punt with her."

"Oh dear," said Sarah. "I hope she knows what she's doing."

"I'm sure she does; you worry too much, my darling," said Rick.

"And you, Ben, have you made any friends?"

"Yes, Mum, but if you mean do I have a special friend

the answer is not really. I was seeing a lot of a girl in Pembroke, but her hobby is wing-walking. She proved a bit too flighty."

Ben laughed, pleased at his own wit.

Rick smiled and managed a grunt of approval.

Later, when they were in bed, Rick said to Sarah that Ben was too sensible to waste time on girls. Sarah told Rick that Ben was still in love with Angelica and in the fullness of time she was sure that they would get together again.

2

Angelica

All my family and friends came down to the Red Jet to see me off. I was feeling anxious and even a bit tearful so it was hard to say good bye to all those people without seeming to be in a hurry to get away, which actually I was. I trundled my huge bag up the gangplank and deposited my overstuffed backpack on the seat beside me. The Red Jet hooted one long blast and moved off. I was in a seat by the window, allowing myself one last look at Cowes. There was Ben was standing on the Parade and waving, like a drowning man. He's waving not drowning I said to myself; I did feel sad: it would be weeks if not months before I would see him again. Alec did not come into it, he didn't cross my mind. It may seem a cruel-hearted thing to say but he had only been a summer romance. I had wanted someone to love; I had needed to find out what that was all about and now I knew. It was no big deal. I felt armed and ready to face a future in Cambridge without the need to rush into a relationship with the first rowing blue I might meet. I would tell this hypothetical person that I had a boyfriend. It would be a lie; Alec had never sent me even a text to let me know how he was getting on in Oxford and when I tried to ring him he never answered. I am sure he is not short of female company, being tall and good-looking. I'm over him but his memory will still come in useful if ever I need an excuse to refuse an invitation.

I went to one freshers' bash and swore never to go to

another. Being surrounded by needy boys put me off. If they look you up and down that's bearable but when they stand too close and start to pat you like you're some kind of animal (a bitch or a pussycat comes to mind) then it's time to make excuses and walk away and if I'm pursued then I call on my relationship with Alec who now turns out to be a heavyweight boxer and insanely jealous. Steady on, I tell myself, if you overdo it you'll lose all credibility.

Then Giles turned up. He didn't look me up and down and he didn't attempt physical contact, at least not at first and by the time he did, I was ready for him.

I had signed up to row in a coxless four, it was a glorious summer's afternoon and we'd had a successful training day, that is until I saw him. Giles was stroke for the Cambridge eight. They had finished before us girls and were sitting in the sun relaxing. As we came alongside I shipped my oar and reached for the pontoon, overbalanced and fell in. I came up spluttering.

"Let me help you," said a male voice, obviously not one of my crew.

"I can manage," I replied, caught hold of the edge and struggled to get out of the water. The next thing I knew a hand had hold of the back of my shirt and I was dumped on the deck.

"There you go," Giles was laughing. I could see his blue eyes twinkling.

After that we seemed to bump into each other frequently in addition to our regular meetings down by the river.

"Hi there, Babe!" he would call out.

I would scowl or laugh depending on my mood.

"I'm not a babe," I would remind him. "I'm a person and I have a name: Angelica."

He soon started calling me Angel, everyone does. I began to feel disappointed if he was not at the boathouse on the afternoon set aside for our training.

Then came the May Ball and Giles made up a party of his friends. I was surprised and flattered to be included.

"What'll you wear?" asked Jane who lived on my staircase.

"I don't know. Is there a dress code?"

"Yes, in a way, floor length silk or satin ball gown and long white gloves."

"OMG I can't do that. I'd feel ridiculous, and I expect I'd look ridiculous too."

In the end I bought a pale blue cotton dress and tied a silk sash around the waist. I didn't get the gloves but I did buy some rather smart high heels. Even then Giles was taller than me. He stayed by my side all evening and when we'd had enough, or in my case too much, to eat and drink, it turned out that Giles was a good dancer. We waltzed around the ballroom in a whirl of heel-leads and spin-turns, then it was the Dashing White Sergeant and we galloped across the floor like we were re-enacting the charge of the Light Brigade.

"Oh help."

I fell backwards into his arms. He caught me so deftly that it looked to those around us as if we had intentionally ended our dance with such a romantic move. With one arm around my waist he escorted me through the French windows and outside onto the terrace. We stepped down onto the grass and out of the bright lights of the ballroom. My high heels sank into the turf so I kicked them off. I felt liberated. Giles stooped to kiss me and I kissed him back just enough to let him know that I wanted him.

That was the beginning of our love affair but I had a lot of work to do and unlike some of the other students I did not miss any lectures and I always went to tutorials.

"I'm not up at Uni to mess about with boys," I told Giles.

"Mess about on the river then; there is nothing half so much worth doing as messing about in boats."

We did a lot of that, rowing on Wednesdays and at week-ends we would take a punt up river to Grantchester.

"Don't expect me to go swimming in the nude. I am not Virginia Woolf."

"And I'm not Rupert Brooke. All that floating about naked and quoting Hamlet is rather old hat don't you think?"

"I'm glad to hear it." I said but could not restrain myself from giving him a kiss. I like Giles, he is quite old-fashioned in some ways and he makes me laugh.

-§-

The long vac was upon us before we knew it. Boats and punts were packed away and students set out on new adventures. I didn't want to be separated from Giles but I had had this offer of a job on a boat in the Mediterranean. His final year was over and he was moving up to London to eat dinners at Gray's Inn.

"It's all part of becoming a barrister: the bar exams,

the dinners and then pupillage."

"Wow, Giles. That sounds worse than school."

"It might be for those that did not thrive at boarding school, but I'm ashamed to say I loved my school days. I'm looking forward to putting on a gown, sitting on a bench at a long oak table eating steak and kidney pie followed by plumb duff. It will be home from home."

I didn't know if he was joking so I gave him a look.

"I really do not want to spend the summer in London," I said.

"What will you do, then?"

"Steve, my Dad's sailmaker friend, is working on a yacht based in the Parma. He tells me they need crew."

"Summer in the Med. That does sound like an offer you should not pass up."

"I've accepted already," I said feeling just slightly guilty that I had not discussed it with Giles beforehand.

"We'll go our separate ways," he sounded rueful.

"But we'll meet again, somewhere, someday," I said and smiled. I had to look away or he would have seen tears in my eyes.

-§-

I went home and took the opportunity to do the RYA course on marine engines. My engineering degree at Cambridge did not cover such practical stuff and I did not want to be stuck in the galley all day, being stuck in the engine room seemed preferable.

While I was on the Island I contacted Ben. He was sailing a Laser now but we borrowed an RS 500 and had a blast. It was as if we had never been apart or stopped sailing together. We had lunch in the club afterwards and I found myself surrounded by old friends. Ben's Dad came over and asked me all about Cambridge. I could see that Ben was listening. He seemed rather quiet as I described rowing and punting. I missed out the bit about swimming at Grantchester. I didn't want his dad asking if I went skinny dipping.

All too soon I was leaving again. Ben was there to see me off.

"What's the yacht you're joining?" he asked.

We hadn't had the chance to talk about my plans for the summer when we were in the club and I, selfishly, had not asked about his.

"Zaca, she's a Grand Banks schooner, owned by some German millionaire. Steve is down there now, sorting out some new sails, but once that's done we'll be heading for the Eastern Med. What'll you be doing?"

"I'm looking forward to sailing my Laser in the GSC regatta and I'm hoping to be doing some sailing in Cowes Week."

"Sounds exciting," I said.

"It's not the same without you," he said "Just remember, I'll still be here when you get back."

I had to hug him. For some reason that I could not fathom, I felt like crying. He's not my brother I told myself so why should I mind leaving him so much? I kissed him on both cheeks and quickly turned away. He was on the Parade as the Red Jet moved out, waving madly just as before.

-§-

I arrived in Parma in time for a farewell dinner for Steve. The owner, Freddie von Braun had taken over half of Le Brasserie du Port for the evening. The Baron rounded up his crew like a German Shepherd, making sure no-one was left behind and all were seated according to rank. His French wife was on his left and Captain Mike was on his right, I managed to squeeze in at the bottom of the table between the cook and Steve. I had a view over the water to where Zaca lay at anchor in the harbour. Just as in Nelson's day the larger vessels seem to prefer to anchor off, I'm not sure why.

"I wonder what we'll be having tonight."

I looked at the slim blued eyed girl on my left. I had only just learnt that her name was Ursula, one of Freddie's many cousins.

"Won't they pass round the menu?" I asked her.

"Certainly not. Freddie will have ordered the meal this morning. We are all his children and he wants to give us a treat, but he doesn't like waiting for his food, and he can't bear all the fuss and indecision that is involved in choosing things from the menu."

"Wow, does he know I'm a Vegan?"

"No! Are you? I'm sure he would never have employed you if he had known that. He can't bear fussy eaters."

Steve started to laugh. Ursula looked confused.

"Angel is no Vegan," he said.

"No I'm not," I had to confess. "I just wanted to see your reaction."

"Angel has a wicked sense of humour," said Steve.

Ursula looked stern but not angry, "Freddie likes to

laugh, but I would not push your luck."

At this point the first course was served and I noticed Freddie had finished his almost before the last plates of crab pâté had been put in front of us humble folk at the bottom of the table.

"Stop fooling about down there," he called out, "or you'll miss out on the next dish. What are you laughing about anyway?"

"Angelica is just being herself, that's all," said Steve. He had to raise his voice to be heard.

"Angelica, stand up and tell us a joke," Freddie called back.

I stood up and leaned forward a bit so I could see him.

"I can't think of a joke just now, but I'll sing you a song, if you like."

"Too late!" cried Freddie. "The sea bass is arriving sit down, please. Songs will come later."

The sea bass was followed by beef en croute which was followed by a sorbet and then cheese and finally fruit. Each course was accompanied by a different wine.

"Oh," I groaned, "I won't need to eat for a week."

"Freddie won't eat tomorrow either," said Ursula and she seemed to be serious.

"Nothing for you to do then," I observed.

"You are quite wrong there," she replied. "Celine only picked at her food tonight, as usual, and the others all expect three meals every day, come hell or high-water, as you English people say."

"I'm surprised they all look so fit," I said.

"That's because it's hard work sailing a schooner, as you will shortly find out," said Steve.

The meal was over and Captain Mike ferried us back

to the ship in the longboat. We sat around on the deck, drinking more wine. I got my guitar and sang *Blue Eyes Crying in the Rain.*

"Sing it again," cried Freddie.

"Sing something else," called Celine.

So I sang *Blue Bayou* for them and then the others joined in with more songs until I thought we would never get to bed.

I said goodbye to Steve on the deck the next morning and watched him zoom away in the tender. It took the next hour to get things stowed away and the sails ready to be hoisted once we had weighed anchor. For authenticity there were no electric winches and every sail had to be raised by turning these huge capture winches. Ursula and I did our bit and by the time we'd finished we were sweating. Once underway Zaca was a magnificent sight as she shouldered her way through the sea; the speed built and the noise of waves slapping the bow increased. The music of the wind in the rigging and the cry of the gulls made tears well up: *this is the life,* I thought.

The crew sat on the bulwarks on the foredeck and the guests who had come aboard that morning clustered around the wheel with their wives and girlfriends. As I had suspected help was needed in the galley and my skills as an engineer were not required. I joined Ursula down below and was surprised when Celine joined us.

"How are you doing?" she asked Ursula in German, changing effortlessly into English when she saw me.

"Pass me the spuds," she said rolling up the silk

sleeves of her blouse, getting ready to peel the potatoes.

I took an instant liking to her.

"Aren't you needed on deck?" asked Ursula. "I mean who is entertaining the guests?"

"Freddie can cope with them. They're boring business men who he needs to impress so that they invest in his next mad scheme."

"But the wives?" I asked.

"Oh they know their place. They'll have stripped off by now and will be posing on the stern-sheets. They're not expected to say anything."

I laughed. "What is his next scheme?"

"I'm sure it's secret, so you must be discrete. It has to do with building a bridge somewhere in Scandinavia, linking an island or even islands to the mainland. It's a huge engineering project."

"That's what I'm studying at Uni." I said.

"Civil Engineering? Interesting. But I wouldn't want even my best friend working for my husband. He's lovely when he's on the yacht but at work he's a ruthless slave driver."

"Last night he made us all feel like family," I said, "even me."

"We are mostly family," said Ursula. "The business men will disembark when we get to Barcelona and then we'll have Zaca all to ourselves."

She was right. In less than twenty four hours we had docked. The Baron went ashore for some sort of civic reception. He was accompanied by Celine and the businessmen and their wives but we, the crew, stayed on board and had an informal supper under the deck awning.

Then the cruise began and we spent days and nights sailing south and east, wafted by moderate breezes, which kept us cool while those on land sweltered in the long hot summer.

"Aren't we going to stop anywhere in Italy?" I asked Ursula.

"Nope, Freddie likes passage making and he doesn't like the Italian coast in summer."

I made a face so she continued:

"But we will anchor off some of the small out-of-the-way fishing villages on the south coast of Sicily."

-§-

We took the tender ashore for fruit and veg, caught fish off the boat and supplemented it with more bought directly from local fishermen. Afternoons were spent swimming and snorkelling around the boat. Some of us tried to harpoon the larger fish. Freddie turned out to be quite a show-off. Celine photographed him climbing up the anchor chain and diving off the boom. The red tiled roofs of an ancient village made a great backdrop.

"Isn't that a bit dangerous?" I asked. "What would we do without the owner?"

"The Captain would make sure we got home safely," Ursula giggled.

"Oh, I see," I said, the realisation dawned on me that my new friend was soft on Mike.

The furious pace of the first few days slowed as we made our way through the Greek Islands. Here the Baron felt at home and we sailed only by day and anchored up each evening in a bay. The smell of thyme and pine needles wafted across the water on the evening breeze. We went ashore to a taverna to eat kebabs, fish and tomato salad. All too soon we reached Marmaris where Zaca was to stay while Freddie and Celine went back to Berlin for work. Captain Mike and Ursula were to remain onboard to supervise the endless round of varnishing and minor repairs that keeps a ship like Zaca afloat. The long vac was coming to an end I had to fly home.

-§-

At Cambridge I got down to work, determined to get a first. It was lonely without Giles and during my second year I spent the odd week-end in London with him. But both of us could see that the relationship was reaching a cross-roads. Either we would get married or we would drift apart. I got the feeling that now that Giles had been called to the bar he needed a regular wife. I had no need of a husband, regular or irregular.

I could see he was going to ditch me when he introduced a friend from home. She was tall, good looking and an accomplished horsewoman, or so Giles told me. I decided to make the first move.

"There is so much going on in Cambridge that I won't be able to make it next week-end," I told him.

He seemed relieved. We kissed goodbye on the station platform and that was the last I saw of Giles.

By the end of my third year I knew I wanted to build bridges. I applied to a firm based in London, was accepted and started work the very next week. There was no break. I got straight down to work. It turned out that the boss knew the Baron. It seemed I had made a valuable contact. But now that I was living in London, I wanted to get out of town at week-ends. I found myself traveling back to the Island and Gurnard Sailing Club.

-§-

"Hi there, Ben."

"What a surprise, Angel. Whose boat have you borrowed this week-end?"

"This time it's a club laser."

We launched and although I had a pretty good start I couldn't keep up with Ben, in fact I was way down the fleet. After the race he helped me drag my boat up the shingle. We took turns washing the dinghies down and putting them away before changing and meeting upstairs in the club. Rick was there.

"Dad is the Gurnard's reigning Grand Master in Lasers." said Ben. "Aren't you Dad?"

"I'm an antique, not a champion. There wasn't much competition."

"Well you beat me today," I said.

"The club boats are OK but the sails are blown, shapeless, in fact useless. You should get your own boat if you're going to be coming down here regularly."

"Are you really able to come down every week-end?" Ben asked.

He seemed pleased even excited at the thought.

"Certainly, for as long as I'm based in London," I replied.

"Then we ought to get a boat we can sail together, like

an RS 500."

"That's an excellent idea," said Rick. "I don't mind chipping in."

Ben looked so happy, which struck a chord in me. I found myself grinning like a fool.

Ben had come down from Oxford and was now teaching in Sandown High School. He had all the summer holidays to look forward to, sailing and mountain biking. It was as if he had never left the Island.

Rick took charge and it was all arranged with such speed that by the following week-end Ben and I were in our new boat. It was just like the old days except that it was Ben who was the helm and I was the crew. Rick bought new sails and Ben polished the bottom, and as a result we were soon back to our winning form. *Together again,* I sang as I bicycled home. I don't know why but I felt happier now than I ever had been in my entire life.

"Will you be down for Dinghy Week?" Ben asked.

It had become almost a routine, these last minute conversations on the way to the Red Jet on Sunday evenings. I didn't need a car in London but now that Ben was living on the Island he had his own battered Volvo estate.

"Of course, I've been granted a week's leave."

"Dad's organising a barn dance and a bar-b-cue for the Saturday night."

"I'll be staying for that," I said.

"Good," he said. "I'm looking forward to sailing with you and dancing the night away."

"You're my best friend," I said and put both arms around him for a long hug and a kiss on both cheeks, French style, before turning to get on the ferry.

I sat down in a seat by the window and as the Red Jet went past the Parade, I could see Ben waving as he always did. I smiled. He's come a long way since we sailed Oppies together, I thought. For a start he's taller than I am now and doing a proper job. I don't know why I couldn't quite acknowledge him as an adult but it was at that moment, sitting on the ferry as it accelerated towards Southampton and my train to London, that I realised he meant more to me than Tori's little brother with whom I went sailing in the holidays. The thought made me feel warm inside. I didn't ask myself where all this might be going.

-§-

"We've got nothing to gain and everything to lose," said Ben as we rigged up for the first race of Dinghy Week.

"What do you mean?" I asked. "We may have won both series to date but that doesn't mean we're bound to win this regatta."

"Everyone will laugh at us if we don't," he replied.

"Well I don't care. There are more things in life than racing sail-boats."

"Not if you live round here," said Ben.

"Why so miserable?"

"Sorry."

"Let's just get out on the water and enjoy ourselves. We don't have to do this for a living."

"Thank goodness," said Ben.

"I know what's got into you," I said "You're cross that you weren't considered for the squad.

"No I'm not," he said.

The way he laughed, I knew I had hit the nail on the head. Ben might be the Laser National Champion but that was a long way from European Champion and nowhere near Olympic Champion. I laughed.

"Anyway," I said. "if you're planning to get to the Olympics you should change classes. What about the 470's?"

"But would you want to sail with me?"

"No, probably not. I certainly don't have the time to go all around the country, up to Scotland and over to the Continent, like the serious sailors. I do have a proper job to go to."

-§-

Needless to say, we did win practically every race in Dinghy Week and loads of cups and mugs and glasses. Ben was pleased and relieved.

"Now you can stop being so grumpy and enjoy the dancing." I told him.

Rick was presiding over the barbecue. He'd wrapped an apron around his waist and was prodding sausages and burgers with some fearsome looking instruments. His face was bright red from the fire and he kept wiping his brow.

"Congratulations Angel," he called as I approached with paper plate in hand.

"You did well yourself," I replied. "Winning the last

race and retaining your title was no mean feat."

He laughed and patted his stomach. "Lucky it was windy. That's when it pays to have plenty of weight in the boat."

"It's skill as well," I said. "Look at me and Ben: we are not giants."

"Ben's grown into a pretty big fellow, I would say," he replied and then added as an afterthought. "Of course you're still a slight little thing, you haven't changed since you were sixteen."

"Rubbish, Rick, I don't know why you want to flatter me. You've known me too long for that."

"That's just why I can. I've known you since you were a nipper."

"Girls can't be nippers, Rick. It's a term reserved for boys on warships in the time of Nelson."

The ceilidh band started. We formed two rings with the girls in the middle and the boys on the outside and began to circle round in opposite directions. I managed to stop opposite Ben so he could swing me round and progress across the floor. The rest of the dance became a chaos of weaving bodies as people bumped into one another; nobody seemed to know where to go. The caller waded in and pushed people in approximately the right direction while singing out "Swing your partner...now do-si-do," all to no avail. At the end of it we collapsed into chairs, or at least I did, while Ben went for more beer.

We wandered outside and along the shoreline, past the beach huts. I found I was holding Ben's hand. He stopped in the shadow of the last hut and put both arms around me. I should have stopped him there and we should have discussed our future in serious tones but I already knew what I wanted and I now realised I had wanted this moment for some time. I put my arms around his neck and kissed him like a lover, tongues and all. Ben didn't seem surprised. It was a long kiss and afterwards we sat on the sea wall, entwined, until I began to get cramp and had to stand up.

"Come on Ben, let's get back to the others."

We wandered along beside the sea to the club but we found the ceilidh band had packed up. Rick and a just few others were putting the barbecue away and generally tidying up. Everyone else seemed to have gone home.

"I think I'm too drunk to drive back to Ventnor," said Ben.

"Yes, you are, and so am I. I'm drunk on your kisses."

"Don't tell anyone."

"Why not?"

Rick understood the situation right away and the three of us walked back to the Pink House. Tori was already home. She didn't seem surprised to see us. She put me in the spare room and Ben slept in his own bed.

Next morning I was up early and went for a run to clear my head. By the time I had showered and changed into clothes Tori lent me, the family had assembled in the kitchen and were having a cooked breakfast.

"Just toast and coffee for me, please."

"Won't you have a croissant?" asked Rick.

I had forgotten Rick's habit of serving up croissants straight out of the oven.

"Well, just for once," and then I added "Thank you very much. It's sweet of you to take so much trouble."

"Where did you two get to last night?" asked Tori.

"We just went for a walk," said Ben

I saw Tori smile at her father like they were sharing a secret.

"I'll run you home later," said Ben.

After breakfast we walked along the front to Gurnard to collect Ben's car. Instead of going to Yarmouth, we headed over to Ventnor and Ben's house. It had belonged to Paul and Tori before they moved back to the Pink House, after Sarah died. Ben lived here now with two other teachers from Sandown High School. I stood at the bedroom window, gazing out over the rooftops towards the Channel.

"On a clear night you can see the loom of the light at Cap de la Hague," said Ben.

He was standing behind me and had his arms around my waist.

"If I lived here I would never close the curtains," I said.

I swivelled round and hugged him.

"I'll never let you go," he said.

I stopped him saying anything else by shutting his mouth with a long wet kiss. While I was busy kissing him, Ben was preoccupied, undressing me. It wasn't difficult, I was only wearing a t-shirt and shorts. We were soon both naked between the sheets.

"You're not Tori's little brother anymore," I said. "You're all mine."

The sun was sinking in the west, filling the room with

a golden light before we surfaced and went downstairs.

"Will you come and live here?"

"Ben, is this a proposal?"

"Yes, it is if you'll say yes."

"Yes, I will."

"Then will you, could we, might we …get married?"

"Don't you think we should wait a bit?"

"For what Angel. We've know each other since we were children. You were so much taller than me that you used to pick me up and swing me round by the straps of my life-jacket."

"I'd almost forgotten those days," I laughed at the memory. Then I added. "The tables have turned now! We'll drive over to Yarmouth to tell my parents tomorrow and then go onto the Pink House to tell your family."

"But tonight I want you all to myself," said Ben.

"I'll phone up for a pizza,"

Ben went off to the cellar to find a special bottle of wine.

-§-

We were married from my home. St James' Church was full of flowers arranged by Mum. The reception was in the Royal Solent Yacht Club. I didn't give up my job in London. I still kept my flat up there in the smoke. That is until I fell pregnant. Amelia was born on a Thursday in the Spring, eighteen months after our Autumn wedding. I'm sure she'll go far.

3

Ginny

The Pink House
Cowes
Isle of Wight

1ˢᵗ September 2021

Dear Grandad,

Where did you go, Grandad? I know you drowned when your old fishing boat sank. But where are you now? I so want to see you. You can't just leave us like this. Mum keeps bursting into tears. It's like she is waiting for you to come through the door. Dad looks so helpless. He doesn't know how to comfort Mum. She's the strong one in this family, or so I thought, but it turns out she depended on you entirely. She's lost without you. We all are. So where have you gone, Grandad? Please come back.

Love
Ginny

PS I've got school tomorrow, so please wish me luck.

-§-

"Ginny, are you asleep?"

Tori pushed the door open a fraction and peered into her daughter's bedroom.

"I can't sleep, Mum."

"Are you worried about school?"

"No Mum, I'm feeling sad. Amelia said ghosts are real and if we believe in them they will visit us."

"Grandad?"

"Yes, Mum. I was hoping if I thought about him very hard that he would come to see me. I never said good bye. He vanished so suddenly."

"I know, my darling. It's hard for all of us."

"I've written him a letter Mum but I don't know his address. So I can't post it."

"Oh, Ginny, that's sweet of you. We'll burn your letter and add it to the ashes in the urn. Then, when we scatter them on the Downs, they will fly up and perhaps he'll be able to read your letter."

"That's a great idea, Mum. Can we do that tomorrow?"

"We'll have to wait until the weekend. Can I read it?"

"No, please don't. It's private."

Next morning Tori dropped Ginny off in Newport to catch the bus to her school in Ryde. It was lunchtime before she could speak to her cousin.

"Have you ever seen a ghost, Amelia?"

"Oh yes! It was in the woods by Newtown Creek."

"Who was it?"

"A drowned sailor. You know that stone monument on the shore just outside the harbour entrance?"

"Yes, we had a picnic on the sandy spit just a little way from there with Mum and Dad, last summer."

"It was one of the boys."

"How do you know?"

"He looked all bedraggled, like he had been washed up on the beach."

"Did he say anything? Did he speak to you?"

"Yes, his voice was very weak and faint, like he was trying desperately hard to get a message to me. It seemed it took all his energy to gasp out a few words."

"What did he say?"

Amelia fixed her green eyes on Ginny and, in a hoarse whisper, said. *"Beware Hamstead Ledge."*

"Oh," said Tori. "Didn't he have any message for his surviving relatives? There must be quite a few here on the Island."

"No," said Amelia. "He just faded from sight."

"Did your mum or dad see him?"

"No, they were too busy with the barbecue."

"Do you think, you could summon him? I so want to see a real ghost. Mum could take us down to Newtown

Creek. She likes sailing with Uncle Ben."

"In Patience? I love that old boat."

"Yes. I've sailed on her nearly all my life. I was only eighteen months old when we went cruising down to Falmouth, with Grandad"

"Could we spend the night at anchor?"

"I'll ask Mum."

-§-

"Ginny, it's time you got dressed. Your uncles will be here in a minute."

"Oh Mum."

It was Saturday morning. Ginny was having a lie-in after a busy week at school. They had burnt the letter and the ashes were in the urn. Tori had invited her brothers to lunch. Ben had returned to the Island and now lived in Ventnor in a house overlooking the sea, once owned by Paul and Tori. Harry was coming down from London. He arrived first. The front door was never locked during the day so he went inside and stood in the hall calling out:

"Hello, Tori, hello Paul! Where's my favourite niece?"

"Here," said Ginny as she descended the stairs, her long blond hair hanging in wet rats' tails around her shoulders. Her brown legs and bare feet stuck out below a cotton dress that she had only just pulled over her head. Harry stooped down and kissed her damp tresses. Amelia came barging into the house:

"Hello Uncle!"

"Ah, my favourite niece!" said Harry.

Ginny went over to Amelia and whispered in her ear. They turned, looked at Harry and burst into giggles.

"You're my favourite niece," they chorused.

"Well, you are both my favourites," said Harry.

Angelica and Ben followed close behind their daughter and Tori came out of the kitchen.

"Lunch is nearly ready. We'll have it in the dining room as there are so many of us. Go through to the garden. Paul will fix you a drink."

Judith was holding a bunch of flowers, standing behind Harry, looking lost. She didn't really know Tori and her family. Tori watched the rest of the party disappear into the garden and then stepped forward to greet her brother's latest girlfriend.

"Good of you to come down, Judith. I know it's a trek getting to the Island."

Paul had brought a table out of the summer house and loaded it with drinks for his guests. Now they stood about the lawn. Ginny and Amelia were on Coca Cola. The adults were drinking wine.

"I hope Harry explained that we're going to scatter father's ashes from the top of the Downs, Judith," said Tori.

"Yes he did, I'm not sure I'll make it up the Downs. I want to be supportive, but I don't want to be in the way."

"You won't be in the way, not at all, but I can see it's awkward for you as you didn't know my dad."

"I might stay here and read a book."

"I quite understand. It's a nice walk along the front to Gurnard, if you feel like a breath of sea air."

Judith smiled. Her pallor and stick like figure

suggested that she might be one of those London girls who are allergic to the seaside.

Tori shepherded her extended family through to the dining room. Betsy had helped her lay out a cold buffet. The brothers and Paul were discussing the city; Tori and Angelica were discussing the arrangements for getting Ginny and Amelia to the next Oppie event, which left Judith rather isolated. The girls were whispering, their heads nearly touching, the salmon left untouched on their plates.

Suddenly, Ginny called out. "Who here believes in ghosts?"

Everyone stopped talking and looked at her. Amelia smiled and put an arm around Ginny.

"I do," said Ben.

"I think we all do," said Tori.

Paul and Harry looked sceptical.

"Depends what you mean," said Paul diplomatically.

"I don't," said Harry. "When people say they've seen a ghost, there is usually a perfectly rational explanation."

"I think people from the past can suddenly pop into your mind when you pass a place that was especially significant to them," said Ben.

"But can you actually see them?" asked Ginny.

"Some people can," said Tori.

"I can," said Amelia. "I saw a ghost in the woods by Newtown Creek."

She squeezed her cousin.

"Can we sail there next week end?" asked Ginny.

"I'll be back in London, I'm afraid," said Harry.

"I've got a lot on just at present," said Paul.

"I'd love a night in Newtown Creek," said Tori.

"I'll come with you," said Ben.

"I'll stay at home," said Angelica. "I've got things to do."

"It'll be just like the old days," said Tori.

-§-

They parked the cars behind the Albion Hotel and walked up the narrow path to the gate that leads out onto Tennyson Down. It is a very steep climb. Harry was panting before they were half way up.

"Judith made the right decision," he gasped.

The girls and their mothers were striding ahead.

"You're not fit, bro," said Ben. "Too much good living," and offered him his arm.

Harry said something rude and Ben jogged after the girls.

They arrived at the Celtic Cross, the memorial to Alfred Lord Tennyson, and waited for Paul to catch up with them. Tori surveyed the scene. The Solent was laid out beneath them; tiny sailing boats seemed to be hardly moving. To the west, in the far distance, the Purbeck Hills were lost in the haze. To the east St Catherine's Lighthouse was a mere dot on the headland. It didn't seem that long ago that they had stood here with Father and scattered Mother's ashes to the wind. Was it really eight years? She handed the urn to Ginny who removed the lid and cast the first handful of ashes into the air; they swirled away towards Freshwater.

"Goodbye Grandad," she murmured. "I'll see you soon," she said under her breath.

Amelia gave her a look, as if she had heard. Then she threw more ashes to the wind. Paul and Ben followed, then Angelica, Harry and finally Tori:

"Rest in peace, Dad."

"Amen," the family responded.

As they were walking back down the hill, Ginny put her arm around Amelia and whispered. "He can't rest in peace until he's come back to see me, so I can say good bye."

"That's right," said Amelia. "Ghosts walk the earth until they have performed all the tasks they left undone when they were alive."

"I'm sure Grandad will come back to see me," said Ginny and a tear rolled down her cheek.

Tori caught up with her and held her close. "Don't cry, darling. He had a very happy life."

She was crying herself.

-§-

With Tori at the helm of Patience, the old gaff cutter, they motored down the Medina River and out into the Solent. She pointed the bows into the wind; Ben went up to the mast to hoist the main. As the sail rose into the air, the brightly varnished spars swung to and fro.

"Mind your heads, girls!" called Tori. But the girls were already crouched down, waiting for the command to sheet in.

They bore away past the Royal Yacht Squadron heading for Newtown Creek. The girls winched in the staysail as it unfurled and finally set the jib.

"No point in hoisting the topsail," said Tori, "with the

tide under us, we'll be there in no time."

She was right. Ben hardly had time to make tea for himself and his sister, before the crew were busy again, furling the head sails and flaking the main in the lazy jacks.

Tori guided them through the narrow entrance. They turned to port and anchored in Clamerkin Lake. Ginny heaved the tender out of its locker and Amelia helped her to inflate it.

"Don't go far girls. I'll start supper in about half an hour."

"We won't, Mum."

They sat side by side on the centre thwart. Each took an oar and they rowed away towards the mouth of the Creek to where a sandbank divides a deep pool from the Solent. It was the place where Tori and her family had picnicked earlier in the Summer. They rowed to the end of the inlet and pulled the tender up on the pebbles.

"It's just along here," said Amelia and led the way to a low stone monument hidden in the coarse sea grass. Beyond this point, dark woods crowded down to the water's edge.

The girls looked at the names.

"I wonder which one you saw," said Ginny. "There's one here called Robert."

"Yes," said Amelia. "I call him Bob."

"Did he say his name?"

"No. But I had a very strong feeling that we had met before, in another life. I knew it was Bob."

"What were you before... before you were Amelia?"

"I was a French pirate, called Amelie."

"Were there other wenches on the pirate ship?"

"Oh yes! We were all armed to the teeth. I fired my pistol at anyone who threatened us."

"Did you kill any dastards?"

"Not as far as I can remember."

Amelia started giggling and Tori joined in. They sank onto the shingle rolling about with laughter.

"Oh dear, Amelia, for a moment I believed you," said Ginny.

"I do believe I had a previous life. But I only know fragments. They come to me in dreams."

They walked back to the dinghy and pushed it into the water.

"If we come back tonight, when the grown-ups are asleep, do you think Bob's ghost will appear?" said Ginny.

"It's quite likely."

"And will I be able to see Bob and talk to him?"

"I hope so. It's possible. I will intercede for you if I can," said Amelia.

-§-

Tori had cooked bangers and mash. As a treat she added a fried egg on top of the potato.

"Hurry up girls, yours is getting cold," she said.

"Where have you been?" asked Ben.

"Only to the spit where people barbecue," said Ginny.

After supper, when the washing up was done, the girls disappeared into the forepeak.

"Don't stay awake all night talking," said Tori and climbed up into the cockpit where Ben was refilling their glasses. Brother and sister sat on opposite sides of the cockpit and watched the sun go down behind the trees, where the rooks were coming in to roost. The swans glided away when they realised that they were not going to be fed. Peace descended on the Creek.

"I think this is the hour Dad loved best," said Tori.

"He did."

They were silent, remembering the old sailor.

"Let's turn in. I'll sleep in the saloon if you take the aft cabin," said Ben.

-§-

The girls took off their shorts but did not get fully undressed. Ginny set her alarm for midnight and put her watch under her pillow so that only she would hear it. She opened the forehatch to its fullest extent and locked it.

"I hope it doesn't rain in the night," she said.

"No chance," replied Amelia.

Ginny thought she would never get to sleep. She lay awake listening to Amelia's regular breathing. She was dreaming of her Oppie when the buzzing of the alarm woke her. She shook Amelia who moaned at first but came to at once when Ginny put a hand over her mouth. They slipped into shorts and jumpers and climbed out of the forehatch, tiptoed down the deck and cautiously lowered themselves into the dinghy. Ginny cast off and sat down beside Amelia. They rowed towards the sandbank that they had reconnoitred earlier. A gibbous moon shone a weak light on the scene from a cloudless sky. It was low tide and the girls struggled to drag the boat up the beach. Ginny took the fisherman's anchor and let out enough warp to embed it in the grass on the top of the bank.

"She's not going anywhere, no matter how much the tide comes in," she said.

They paused and looked around at the calm sea reflecting the starlight. The seaweed left by the retreating tide gave a salty tang to the night wind. The ebb and flow of the tide sucked at the shingle.

"Shiver me timbers," said Amelia.

"What?"

Ginny turned and looked towards the gravestone. The phosphorescence gliding over the water could almost be mistaken for a human shape. At that moment the sea made a gurgling sound, like someone heaving a deep sigh.

"Beware the reef."

"Bob? Bob is that you?" whispered Amelia.

Ginny shuddered and grabbed her cousin's hand. She was about to ask Bob if he had seen Grandad when the stillness was broken by the distant thunder of powerful marine engines. The girls looked up to see a motor cruiser ablaze with lights heading towards them. It was still a long way off but it was travelling at speed.

"What's that gin palace doing here?" asked Amelia.

"People who own that sort of boat often party all night. I expect they're coming back from Lymington," said Ginny, hoping her cousin would be impressed by her intimate knowledge of the party set. Amelia didn't have time to call Ginny's bluff.

"It's heading straight for the reef!"

"I'll get the torch, Mum always keeps one in the dry

bag." said Ginny and raced back to the dinghy.

She opened the bag, grabbed the torch and ran back along the spit. Amelia took it from her and started flashing out an SOS.

"It's the only signal I know. At least it should make them stop and think."

"That's if anyone is looking out."

"Right! If they're on autopilot, they've had it!"

The roar of the massive diesel engines grew louder every second; the lights blinded them as the enormous vessel came closer and closer. It clipped the Hamstead Buoy with a clang that echoed across the Solent and woke Tori in her bunk. Then it hit the ledge with the noise of metal being torn into strips by an enormous force.

-§-

The girls stood stock still and stared as the cruiser came to rest on its side, half out of the water. The lights went out and there was complete silence. Then, as their night vision returned, they saw two shadowy figures emerge from the water and struggle up the beach. Ginny felt Amelia grip her hand. She stifled a scream.

"Oh my God," whispered Amelia.

"Ghosts?"

"Bob?" called out Amelia. "Is that you?"

"No, it's Christine and Mandy. Please help us, please."

"Come back to Patience and we'll call for help," said Ginny. "We can't do anything here."

"Come on," said Amelia and took Christine by the

hand. "We need to get you back to the boat as quick as we can."

With Christine in the bows and Mandy perched on the transom the girls rowed as hard as they could.

Ginny held the dinghy steady while the two shipwrecked girls climbed aboard Patience. She handed the painter to Amelia who made fast.

"Mum," she shouted.

"Dad," shouted Amelia.

"Emergency!" they both yelled at once.

Tori and Ben appeared in the cockpit.

"What the hell…" started Ben.

"Where have you come from?" asked Tori.

Ginny was already at the VHF radio. "Mum we have to put out a Mayday. A cruiser has hit the ledge and these people swam ashore. But there must be others… maybe trapped…"

Tori took the handset from her.

"Mayday relay. Mayday relay. Mayday relay. This is Patience, Patience. My position is Clamerkin Lake. The casualty is on Hamstead Ledge. Over."

Christine and Mandy were still in their bikinis. They were shivering, teeth chattering. Ben ushered them below and started handing out dry clothes. He put the kettle on the hob.

"Patience this is Solent Coastguard. Name and position of boat in distress. Over"

Tori looked at the two teenagers.

"Name of your boat?"

"Bat Out of Hell," answered Christine.

"Solent Coastguard, Patience. Bat Out of Hell. On the Hamstead Ledge. Over."

"Patience. Solent Coastguard. Number of people on board? Over."

Again Tori looked at the teenagers.

"Hundreds," answered Mandy.

"No, not hundreds. Maybe twenty. Certainly more than ten," said Christine.

"Solent Coastguard. Patience. We have two of the passengers on-board Patience. There are between ten and twenty people left unaccounted for. Over."

"Patience. Solent Coastguard. Please stand by the casualty and listen out on Channel 16 for further instructions. Lifeboats are on their way. Over."

"Listening out," replied Tori.

Ben handed round mugs of tea. The two older girls sat side by side on the Ben's bunk. Ginny and Amelia sat opposite them. Mandy stopped shivering and stared back at Ginny.

"What are you looking at?"

"Sorry," said Ginny. "I was just wondering why you were in your bikinis in the middle of the night? Did you plan on going for a swim?"

"The same thought occurred to me," said Ben. "What were you doing on that boat?"

"Modelling. That's what we do," said Christine.

"Fascinating. But we'll have to hear all about it later," said Tori. "We need to up anchor and stand off Hamstead Ledge as the Coastguard instructed."

Leaving their guests in the saloon, Tori and Ginny started the engine while Ben and Amelia went forward and worked the windlass.

"It's up. You can motor forwards," Ben called to Tori.

"We'll clean the mud off the deck later," he told Amelia.

They stood in the bows shinning the torch to help Tori avoid the mooring buoys in their path. Patience negotiated the narrow channel and motored towards the cardinal mark well to the east of Hamstead Ledge buoy. They could see the wreck only a few hundred yards away. The Yarmouth lifeboat was already on the scene. As they watched, the Cowes inshore lifeboat arrived.

Tori got onto the VHF. "Mayday relay, Solent Coastguard this is Patience, Patience. Over"

"Patience. Solent Coastguard. There are multiple casualties still on-board the Bat Out of Hell. It's too shallow for the Yarmouth boat to approach the vessel so the inshore lifeboat will be transferring them. If your two passengers are stable then proceed to Yarmouth where ambulances are gathering. Over."

"Solent Coastguard. Patience. Understood. Proceeding Yarmouth. Listening out on Channel 16."

Two heads appeared in the companionway.

"May we come up, please?" said Christine.

They squeezed into the cockpit. Ginny moved up for them and Amelia sat down opposite. Ben was keeping a look out, Tori was at the helm.

"I've never met a real model," said Ginny. "Do you often have to do it at night?"

"Yea," said Mandy. "Sometimes at night, sometimes at midday."

"Sometimes on a beach in the sun and sometimes on a yacht at dusk," said Christine. "It's whatever who's paying wants."

"And whatever he thinks will sell the clothes, swimsuits, whatever," said Mandy.

"You two should try it when you're a bit older," said Christine.

"It pays well, if you play your cards right," said Mandy.

"Oooh," said Amelia, "that sounds interesting."

The survivors of the shipwreck looked at each other and started to giggle. To Tori they didn't seem much older than the girls.

"It's a job not without its dangers, I should think, judging by what happened tonight," she said.

"You're right there," said Mandy. "If we hadn't crashed I was thinking of jumping overboard when we stopped."

"Is that why you were still in your bikini?" asked Amelia.

"Partly," said Christine, "and partly because the men had thrown our clothes overboard."

"Oh gosh! Why did they do that?" asked Ginny.

"They weren't very nice," said Mandy.

Tori interrupted before anymore revelations could surface. "Lucky the girls found you. I still don't know why they were on the spit when you came ashore. What were you doing, girls?"

"Amelia saw a ghost," said Ginny.

"Yes," said her cousin. "I knew we would. It was just before the crash."

"Really?" It was Mandy's turn to look surprised. Her eyes were huge. She lent forwards. Christine looked cool. Ghost stories were clearly not her thing.

"I was going to ask Bob if he could put me in touch with Grandad," said Ginny.

"And did he?" Mandy seemed anxious to know.

"There was a strange light on the water. It looked like a person," said Ginny.

"Then I heard his voice, and I knew it was Bob," said Amelia.

"The boy who drowned on Hamstead ledge years and years ago," explained Ginny.

"What did he say?" said Mandy.

"*Beware the ledge,*" said Amelia. "It's like he tries to warn sailors to avoid the ledge."

"But often, they ignore him, it would seem," said Tori. "Now girls get ready to moor up. We'll be port side to."

They rounded the end of the pier and glided into the harbour. The flashing lights of three ambulances were illuminating the quay in cold blue colours.

All four girls jumped up and the cousins got warps and fenders out of the cockpit lockers.

"Can we help?" said Mandy.

"What shall we do?" asked Christine.

"You ladies just sit still until we are safely tied up," said Ben.

The girls took the ropes and secured them to the cleats on the pontoon while Ben went to talk to the paramedics.

"Well ladies, it seems the paramedics have orders to take you to casualty for a check-up. I did tell them that you seem remarkably fit to me. But it seems orders is orders."

The rescued girls started to undress.

"Please, no need, you can keep the clothes. They're only old boating rags," said Tori.

"We're not as mean as your boyfriends on the gin palace," said Ben.

"Boyfriends!" said Mandy. "They thought they had

got us trapped! Thank goodness for that great big rock."

"Yes. Yes. You've escaped with your virtue intact. It been nice meeting you, now follow Ben he'll show you where to go," said Tori.

As Mandy stepped ashore she whispered to Ginny. "If you do find your grandad, please let me know. I just lost my nan and I so what to see her again for one last time."

Ginny nodded. "I will."

With Ben back on the boat, they slipped the lines and motored back to Newtown Creek.

"Now girls we're going to have a nice long lie-in in the morning," said Tori.

"And no more ghost hunting," said Ben.

"Promise?" said Tori.

"We promise," said the girls.

But they did look sad, Ginny especially. They crept into the forepeak, undressed and got into their bunks.

"Good night, Amelia," whispered Ginny.

"Sleep tight," came the muffled response.

Ginny lay staring into the darkness for a few minutes before exhaustion overwhelmed her.

-§-

The darkest hour is just before dawn. The cabin was stuffy; Ginny was restless, half out of her sleeping bag. She rolled over and nearly fell off the bunk. Strong hands pushed her back into the middle and tied up the lee cloth.

"Good night, my bird," whispered a gravelly voice. "I'm watching over you. You did well to rescue those two wayward creatures. I won't say good bye as I'll always be around, just out of sight, so don't be sad."

-§-

The pale light of dawn filtered into the cabin. Amelia stirred.

"Hey Ginny, when did you put up your lee cloth?"

Ginny's tousled head appeared over the canvass.

"What? I never did that. But I did have a lovely dream. Grandad came and spoke to me. He said. *Well done for saving the girls.*"

"And tied up the lee cloth," said Amelia.

She climbed out of her bunk and got in with Ginny.

"Ghosts really do exist, just as I said."

She smiled and gave Ginny a kiss.

-§-

It was hours later when Tori peered into the forepeak. The girls were fast asleep. As she bent over them, Ginny opened one eye.

"Morning, darling."

"What time is it?"

"Ten o'clock. You've been asleep for hours. Did Amelia spend the whole night in your bunk?"

"No," said Amelia. "I got in when Ginny said she'd seen a ghost."

"Yes, Mum. I really did see a ghost."

Tori sat down on the edge of the bunk, smiled and prepared to listen.

"It was Grandad. I was falling out of bed. He pushed

me back in and tied up the lee cloth, so that I'd be safe."

"How do you know it was Grandad?"

"It wasn't me," said Amelia.

"He said, *Good night, my bird.* Grandad is the only one who ever called me that."

"Did he say anything else?" asked Tori, blinking away tears.

"Yes, he said, *I'm watching over you.....don't be sad.*"

"He said, *Well done for saving those two girls.* Didn't he?" asked Amelia.

"Yes he did," said Ginny. "It was his voice alright, low and gravelly."

Tori leaned forward and hugged Ginny, Amelia tried to put her skinny arms around both of them.

"Oh darling," whispered Tori. "I wish I could have seen him."

-§-

The smell of frying bacon filled the boat. Ben put his head through the door.

"What's happening here? Has someone died?"

"No Ben, we're remembering Grandad. His spirit seems to haunt this old boat," said Tori.

"It was the thing he loved most. No doubt about that," said Ben. "Come along and have breakfast. I'm sure that'll make you feel better."

"Thank you, Ben," said Tori.

"We'll never sell Patience, will we, Mum?"

"No, never, darling. How could we?"

Photo by John Green, Cowes.

4

Stevie

They met in Dingwall's Dance Hall; the band was coming to the end of a session.

Black Mountain people,
They uses gunpowder
Just to sweeten their tea.

George Melly finished the number and collapsed into an armchair placed on stage just for him.

Quentin turned to the girl who was also propping up the long bar:
"Hi, Dolly, can I buy you a drink?"
The Dolly Parton blond wig, black leather jacket and Doc Martens scowled at him.
"My name is not Dolly."
They stared at each other, the seconds ticked by, neither of them smiled. Either we are soul-mates; our star signs are compatible and she'll say yes, or I'm wrong and she'll say no, thought Quentin.
"But if you must," the girl continued. "I'll have a Tequila Sunrise."
Quentin signalled to the barman: "Two Tequila Sunrises, please."
"What's your star sign?" asked the girl.
"Tell me your name first," said Quentin.
"Stevie."
"Gemini."

"Two faced. Never trust a Gemini."

"Says who?"

"My mother."

"Ah. She didn't say: one face looks to the past to inform the other who looks to the future?"

"No, but she did say they could be fun. My dad was a Gemini."

"Where is he now?"

"I don't know; he's long gone."

They drank in silence for a while. Another band was playing.

"Fancy a blast on the old Harley; you're dressed for it."

"The leather trousers, you mean?"

"Yes. They'll certainly help if you go skidding along the road on your back side."

"They're not the real thing. I wouldn't trust them to save my skin."

"Where would you like to go?"

"Where in the world, do you mean?"

"No, we're limited to England."

"I'm all dressed up with nowhere to go. You choose."

"I've a cottage on the coast near Warkworth."

"Where's Warkworth?"

"County Durham."

"That's miles away!"

"Yep, about 300 miles. If we leave now we'll be there by morning. What are you doing tomorrow?"

"Nothing. I ain't doing nothing and I ain't got nothing."

"And nothing to lose?"

"That's about it."

Leaving the old warehouse, they passed George Melly's table.

"Night, Quentin," called George. "Have a good one!"

"Night George," Quentin raised a hand in salute.

They went round the corner to where the Harley Davidson was propped on its stand by the canal. The street lights left glittering reflections on the still water.

"Is Quentin really your name?"

"Yes Stevie, it really is."

"The Quentin? The sax player."

"The very same."

He pushed the Harley upright and mounted.

"Hop on."

Stevie put a boot on the rear foot rest and swung up onto the pillion. Her movements were smooth and easy, like she had done this before. The engine was making a low rumble, barely ticking over as they inched out of the yard, and onto Chalk Farm Road, heading for Golders Green and the beginning of the Great North Road.

"Hold on tight. We'll blast on through the night."

His shout was carried away by the wind and drowned by the roar of the engine. He kept the speed down until they were out in the countryside then he wound her up. They were doing the ton.

"Just for kicks," he yelled.

Stevie let go the steel bar behind her seat, put her arms around his waist and hung on. He was singing but she couldn't make out the words or the tune. If she had cared to look she would have seen the faded red letters on the back of his leather jacket which spelled out the words:

Too old to die young.

"Slow down Quentin," she shouted. "If you don't stop for a rest we'll crash and I'm too young to die."

They pulled into a lay-by where a caravan that had once been white, was serving breakfast out of a long narrow hatch. Truckers, bikers and hitch hikers were gathered round eating: plate in one hand, fork in the other. Quentin ordered for both of them:

"Egg, sausage, fried bread and beans, please."

Stevie corrected him. "I'll have tomatoes and no beans, please." She smiled at the woman behind the counter.

They drank hot sweet tea out of chipped white mugs. There was just one teaspoon, chained to the counter.

"Go easy on the beans, Quentin."

"Blazing saddles! I'll eat what I want."

He got a flask out of one of the saddle bags and poured a tot of whisky into his tea.

They went roaring down country lanes and came at last to a fishing village. Quentin's cottage was up a narrow cobbled alley. Stevie showered and Quentin cooked up an omelette.

They piled into the double bed that filled the entire space of the only bedroom. Quentin fell asleep immediately. It was evening when he was woken by Stevie caressing his nipple. She swung a leg over him and mounted; her movements were smooth and easy, like she had done this before.

Later, they walked down to the wharf; the cold, salty wind stung their faces. The Anchor pub had small windows more to keep the elements at bay than to take in the sweeping views of the North Sea. The local fishermen seemed to know Quentin; they regaled the newcomer with tales of times gone by; good times, when the herring fleet had numbered one hundred boats and there were plenty of fish to go round. The wives had spent days and nights filleting and smoking the catch.

Quentin left the cottage at dawn. He didn't wake Stevie, she looked so peaceful lying there, all snuggled down under the duvet. He walked along to the quay where his old wooden fishing smack was moored. He only planned to be out a few hours. He thought what fun it would be to surprise Stevie with freshly caught fish for lunch but as always it all took much longer than he had planned. When he got back Stevie was gone. She had left a note on the kitchen table.

You're a queer fish, old man.
You belong to the sea.
I'll set you free,
I'll set you adrift.
You'll go west.
The sinking sun
will be your companion.
If there is another shore,
we'll meet there.

-§-

Quentin had not expected to see Stevie again. One-night-stands are best left that way, he reflected, as he made his way down to Oxford for a gig. The jazz band was meeting in the Jericho Tavern. Their regular tenor sax had been taken ill so at the last moment somebody had thought of Quentin.

"Hi, glad you could make it."

Dave, the lead singer, was leaning against the bar. Beside him stood a slim girl with short black hair wearing an embroidered kaftan over blue jeans.

"Stevie?"

"Quentin?"

"I didn't recognise you without the wig."

He smiled and held out a hand. Stevie did not take his hand. She scowled.

"I didn't recognise you without the leathers."

"I left them in the hotel. They're too hot for a night like this."

Dave laughed. "Don't tell me you're going to work up a sweat playing that sax. I've had a bed put on the set just in case you fall asleep during our gig."

"You're joking, at least I hope you are."

"How do you two know each other?"

"We don't," they said in unison, as if they had rehearsed the line. There was a pause while Dave looked from one to the other.

"Fine, I don't want to come between old friends; I'll go and find the boys. We won't be starting the first set for a while."

He left to find the other two musicians and set up the stage at the back of the pub.

"What are you doing here, Quentin."

"Doing my thing: sax."

"But why here and now? Of all the pubs in England and all the bands, you turn up here on my turf."

"Well, this isn't the Turf and Dave is an old friend. When John dropped out he rang me up. So I quit fishing and came right over. Didn't he tell you?"

"No. At least, he did say he'd found a replacement for John but he didn't say it was you."

"There's only one Quentin, but if you're offended then I'll go back to sea."

Stevie considered for a second then she smiled.

"Don't go Quentin. We're going to have some fun."

"Are you sharing vocals with Dave?"

"Maybe."

"Songs you've written?"

"Maybe."

"You're going to be hot in that kaftan."

"I won't be wearing it on stage."

"Can I get you something?"

Stevie nodded. "Whisky, please."

Quentin ordered a pint for himself and a chaser for Stevie. They took their drinks to the back of the pub to meet the rest of the group. Quentin knew them all; he'd been around a long time. They greeted him with nods and smiles.

"Hi man."

"Good to see you, man."

"Do you know Stevie? She's cool, written a load of new stuff."

Quentin just nodded. He left it to Stevie to tell the boys that they had met before.

"Just do your thing, don't you, darlin'," said Dave.

He put his arm around her and pulled her close. Quentin got his instrument out of its case, so that's the way it crumbles he thought.

They jammed for about thirty minutes, Quentin just followed the others and did his solo when the baritone sax swung round towards him. Stevie rattled a tambourine but she didn't sing. When Dave was satisfied that they all knew what they were doing he called a halt and they moved to a table in the far corner and ordered food.

"Venison pie for me, please," Quentin said to the girl behind the bar.

"How could you?" asked Stevie and ordered the vegan option.

"I'm sure the deer led a happy life, and it would be a waste not to eat it. Besides, it's a treat. Venison isn't generally on the menu."

"It isn't a treat to be shot by one bastard and then eaten by another," said Stevie. She sounded serious.

"Is it because you're vegan you didn't stay to eat the lovely fish I caught, all those months ago?"

"No. I was bored. Didn't know where you'd gone or when you'd return so I took the train back to London."

"Bored in Warkworth? How could you say that about a place with such a rich history?"

"You are joking, Quentin. I was the fish out of water. I've never felt the need to get back to London so urgently."

"But you're in Oxford now. What are you doing here?"

"Finishing my degree. This is my last year."

"What are you reading?"

"Engineering"

Quentin looked at her over the rim of his beer glass.

He saw her in a new light. He winced. I should have taken more care of her, not just assumed I could pick her up and drop her like she was just another fish in the sea, just another trophy for the man with the rod, just another notch on the bedpost.

They re-joined the others at the table. Stevie went to sit beside Dave. Quentin engaged two of the other musicians. It turned out that one was reading Mathematics and the other Physics. The pub was starting to fill up and it was time for the band to start their first set.

Stevie jumped up on the stage and pulled her kaftan over her head. She was wearing a boob tube, high fashion in some circles, but it still took Quentin by surprise. He tried not to notice her nipples, regretting again that he had been so callous.

"Welcome and thank you for joining us this evening," Dave smiled at the audience, who were starting to gather round the low stage.

"We're going to start with a new number, written by Stevie here. Put your hands together for the latest edition to our band."

People clapped. Stevie bowed and the baritone sax played a scale. Then they were away; Dave and Stevie's harmonies complementing each other like they'd done this many times before. The song sounded angry and if you listened to the words, Stevie seemed to be accusing Dave of two-timing her:

You do your thing man, and I'll do mine.
But don't you cry and wail, when I'm gone.

Dave had the next two lines:

You do your thing baby, and I'll do mine.
If we meet again, darling, that's just cool.

Quentin didn't believe a word of it, but it made him smile.

He was packing away his sax when Stevie came over.

"Where are you staying?"

"At the Randolph."

"Wow, that's posh."

"I sold a lot of fish."

"Liar. You wouldn't recognise a herring if it jumped up and bit you."

"OK. I've written some stuff and I've been playing with a band in Newcastle that's signed a contract with Decca."

"OK! Now I don't know if you're lying or not."

"Leave me out of it. It seems fortune's favoured you since London. What happened to the little waif and stray I met all those months ago."

"You're so free with compliments, Quentin. I should slap you for calling me a sad cat. But I'll humour you."

"I never said you were sad! You told me you had nothing and nowhere to go!"

"I just fancied you. I knew if I played helpless that would get you going."

"Why don't we meet up at my hotel for lunch tomorrow? We might to get to know each other a bit better."

"I never hit the streets before noon."

"Well if you manage to crawl round to the Randolph

by one I'll treat you."

"Beans you mean, I expect. Still a girl's got to keep body and soul together somehow. I'll be there."

-§-

It's not far from Somerville to the Randolph Hotel and Stevie walked through the doors at exactly one o'clock. Quentin was lounging in a comfortable chair in the foyer, pretending to read the papers.

"That's an amazing dress, Stevie."

Stevie looked surprised. "You noticed?"

"It floats round you like a cloud round a goddess."

Stevie frowned. "Steady on, Quentin. I don't want you having apoplexy before lunch. Sober up and show me to the dining room."

They ate in silence. Stevie didn't comment on the food (Beef Wellington) or the wine (a fine claret), but she swallowed it all down as if she hadn't eaten for days. Quentin watched her. She wiped her mouth and lifted her glass to be refilled, again:

"Cheers Quentin. I'm ready for your absurd compliments now."

"What were you doing in London, if you weren't down on your luck with nowhere to go?"

"It was the long vac and I was staying with my mother."

"So you were bored?"

"No. I was having a whale of a time. Men calling me every day and promising all sorts of daft and extravagant things."

"So you took off to the North Country with me. Why?"

"Well you were the only one who didn't seem complicated. My mother was almost ready to start fitting me out in a wedding dress."

"I'm simple soul."

"How do you spell that?"

"Sole."

Stevie nodded. "I'm good at Maths, and I can understand engineering principles, but spelling is not my strong point."

"Maybe we do have something in common then. I haven't met many female engineers. Any particular field interest you?"

"I'd like to be a yacht designer."

"Shouldn't you be reading Naval Architecture?"

"Possibly, but I reasoned that Engineering gave me more options if yacht design didn't work out. And Oxford doesn't offer Naval Architecture."

"How did you get into yachting?"

"I've been crewing for a school friend's father."

"What boat's he got?"

"Nicholson 48: a classic. She's quick. We won the Royal Escape race to Fécamp."

"Where does he keep her?"

"Brighton marina. I was at school near there and my friend lives in Rottingdean."

"A girl friend?" asked Quentin.

"Yes, and it was a girls' school. No boys allowed." Stevie laughed.

"There's a great tradition of yacht building in New Zealand."

"I'd love to go to New Zealand, one day," said Stevie.

"Maybe you will, and maybe I'll come with you."

The conversation came to a halt and Quentin ordered coffee.

"Do you fancy an afternoon punting?" asked Stevie.

"Just the two of us?" asked Quentin.

"Three would be a crowd, don't you think?"

They left the hotel and walked up St Giles towards the Cherwell Boathouse.

They went upstream towards the Vicky Arms. Stevie lay back on the cushions and watched as he heaved the long pole up into the air before dropping back into the water.

"OK Quentin, let me show you how it's done."

They changed places and the punt shot forward, but it seemed to Quentin that Stevie was trying too hard. She was getting soaked as the water ran down the pole and then her arms. Her cotton summer dress was soon transparent, her nipples prominent.

"I'm enjoying this Stevie."

"You lazy hound."

"The wetter your dress becomes the more you look like Josephine."

"Explain."

"In Napoleon's Paris, fashionable ladies wore very light cotton dresses, just like yours, and sprayed themselves with water to make the material cling to their bodies. You would not have looked out of place, in your chemise."

"You're too weird, old man. You're old enough to be my father. You shouldn't be noticing my charms."

"I'm not, in fact, quite that old and I'd have to be made of stone not to appreciate your nearly naked form."

They approached the meadow below the pub. Quentin stepped ashore and tied up while Stevie tried to shake the water off her dress, like a dog coming out of the river.

"You'll have to take it off and ring it out," suggested Quentin.

"No thank you, I'll just lie here in the sun and dry off while you get in the drinks. It's cider for me."

Quentin made his way up the slope to the Vicky Arms, by the time he got back, Stevie was gently steaming. He sat down beside her.

"What will you do when exams are over and you've got your degree?"

"I've got a few ideas. There's a Japanese shipyard that has offered me a job. I would be in the design office. They would give me time off for further studies at the University in Tokyo."

"Do you speak Japanese?"

"No Quentin, but I expect I could learn. It can't be that hard to get the basics."

Quentin raised his eyebrows but said nothing. So Stevie went on:

"On the other hand I have also been offered a place in Brittany designing and building racing yachts."

Quentin nodded. "The French build the best offshore boats in the world. But do you speak Breton, Stevie?"

"Even in Brittany they speak French, and I am fluent."

"You're a girl of many talents, that's for sure."

Quentin heaved a sigh.

"What's the big sigh for? Aren't you happy, old man."

"You've got it in one Stevie. I'm old, *too old to die young,* and I've messed things up, while you seem to be on the brink of a wild adventure."

She put an arm around him, brushed the hair out of his eyes and looked into his face.

"You told me you and your band are playing gigs; have signed up with a record company and are making money. What more could a musician want?"

"You."

He pulled her to him, rolled her over and put his lips to her ear.

"Be my, be my baby tonight."

They returned the punt to the Cherwell Boathouse. Stevie said she had to call in at Somerville to get a change of clothes. Quentin went back to the Randolph and advised the desk clerk that he would be staying another night. He sat on the bed, waiting for Stevie. Then on an impulse rang down for a bottle of Champagne and a seafood platter. After staring at the trolley for what seemed like an hour he gave in, poured himself a drink and started nibbling on a prawn.

It was getting dark when he gave up waiting for her and rolled into bed. I knew she wouldn't show, he thought, as he fell asleep. He dreamt of Stevie running through the long grass below the Vicky Arms.

Someone was a pounding on the door of his room. Quentin rolled over and looked at his watch. It was past midnight. He found a towel, tied it around his waist and went to see what the racket was about.

"Stevie?"

"Yes, Quentin it's me. Sorry I'm late."

"Glad you could make it."

He gave her a brief hug but then turned and went back to bed, throwing the towel onto the floor. Stevie shut the door behind her and undressed. The next thing Quentin knew she was wrapped around him, kissing the back of his neck. He struggled to roll over and somehow she finished up astride him, leaning forwards and pressing her lips to his lips.

It was only the next morning that Quentin noticed Stevie had a black eye.

"How did you get that shiner. Was that me?"

He was about to apologise.

"No Quentin. It wasn't you. Order up some breakfast and I'll explain, once I've had something to eat."

They sat up in bed with the breakfast tray across their knees, eating in silence. Quentin poured more coffee and put the tray down on the floor.

"It was that bastard Dave."

"My friend Dave?"

"My boyfriend Dave. But now…"

Stevie pulled a finger across her throat indicating that Dave was now history.

"Why?"

"I went back to my room and he was waiting for me. He accused me of sleeping with you, complained I didn't love him. I said: "fine, let's leave it like that then." He said: "but why? Is Quentin so much better in the sack than I am?" I just laughed; that seemed to upset him. He called me a bitch and slapped me. I hit him back and then he punched me."

"Ah, nothing too serious then."

"Not in the great scheme of things, I suppose, but I still feel sad it had to end like that."

"Is it over?"

"Yes, Quentin. It's over between me and Dave."

"You're not going to be singing with him?"

"No. You're not going to play in the band either."

"Really?"

"Yes, Dave is coming to kill you Quentin."

"No. He's my old mate."

"Not anymore."

"What is it about you and men, Stevie? What's all the drama about?"

"Beats me Quentin. But I think we better split."

It was only then that he noticed Stevie's backpack on the floor, and her leathers piled on a chair.

"I'll just shower first, if you don't mind," said Quentin.

"We'll shower together. Save time and water."

Quentin smiled. There isn't anyone quite like Stevie, he thought. I can see why Dave might be upset.

Quentin went down to the desk and paid the bill, then he left the hotel by the back exit that led into the yard where the Harley Davidson was parked. Stevie was waiting. He pushed the machine off its stand and kicked it into life. Stevie put a boot on the foot rest and swung up behind him. Quentin edged the machine out of the yard, into the street and turned left onto St Giles. It was then that he noticed a mini following them. It passed them on the Woodstock Road and then braked suddenly. The car door was flung open and Quentin could see

Dave struggling to get out. He swerved round him and turned into Rawlinson Road, then left onto the Banbury Road and accelerated. He could hear Stevie shouting in his ear:

"GO, Quentin GO."

They were heading for the M40. The mini kept up the chase for a few miles, but it was not able to overtake traffic with the same agility as the bike and by the time they were on the motorway it was far behind. They were doing the ton. Quentin was singing and Stevie had her arms around his waist, squeezing him tight. After a while he left the busy road and headed north and west into Wales. They stopped in Shrewsbury, for lunch.

"Where are we going to stop for the night?"

"Where would you like to spend the night, Stevie?"

"By the sea, Quentin."

"Aberystwyth, then. Do you speak Welsh?"

"No, I don't."

"It's very like Breton."

"You're a fund of irrelevant information."

-§-

The hotel was on the seafront not far from Mario Rutelli's war memorial. They signed in and went up to their room. Standing at the window, they looked out across the Irish Sea where a trawler was slowly making its way towards the port. Quentin was standing behind Stevie; he put his arms around her.

"We should go down to the harbour and see what they've caught."

Stevie wriggled free and reached up to kiss him. They

grabbed their jackets and went out into the street, along the promenade and past the statue of Winged Victory. On the top of the monument a girl in a billowing gown was holding a laurel wreath. At the base a naked figure was struggling out of a hedge of thorns.

"Isn't she beautiful?" said Quentin.

"If you like that sort of thing," replied Stevie.

"Humanity emerging from the Horrors of War," he read.

Stevie shook her head.

"So many boys senselessly slaughtered. The politicians could have ended it all much sooner than they did. The generals would not have objected."

"How do you know that?"

"Siegfried Sassoon. It's all in his poems and in his autobiography."

"I know the poems but I didn't know that."

"Georgian poetry was my thing at Roedean, Quentin. I did A level English."

"So you changed tack after leaving school?"

"Yes. To get Maths and Physics I had to go to a crammer in Brighton."

"Ah, Brighton days," said Quentin.

Stevie looked at him out of the corner of her eye, but said nothing. They came to the walled harbour. The tide was ebbing fast and a fishing boat was leaning up against the quay. The crew were unloading their catch and women were packing the fish into boxes already half filled with ice. Stevie approached the person in charge.

"You can have two bass and a few langoustine," said the fisherman's wife. She half-filled a plastic bag with the crustaceans and put two fish on top.

"Thank you, thank you, thank you very much. That is so kind." Quentin and Stevie were so happy that their chorus of appreciation sounded a bit like seagulls fighting over scraps.

Back at the hotel, the kitchen staff said it was no trouble at all to cook the seafood, and Stevie gave them half the langoustine in return.

"Leave me up here, Quentin. I want to change into something more comfortable. I'll join you in the bar."

"OK. What'll you have?"

"You choose."

Quentin went down and asked the barman for a bottle of white wine and, after a pause for thought, two glasses of sweet sherry.

"Bristol Cream?" asked the man.

Quentin nodded and gave him his room number. His back was turned towards the door. All at once the room went silent. Someone let out a low whistle and the barman seemed to forget what he was doing as Stevie walked into the room in a long silk dress. It was as if Ingrid Bergman had just walked into Rick's Bar.

"Wow, Stevie! I never..." Quentin began.

Stevie curtsied.

"You never what?" she asked.

Quentin was speechless.

"You never thought I owned a dress?" she was laughing.

"What'll you have?"

Stevie eyed the sherry suspiciously.

"One Tequila Sunrise, please," she said to the barman.

"Coming right up!" said the man, American

overcoming his usual Welsh accent.

They moved through to the dining room. The cook had whisked up a Hollandaise sauce to go with the langoustine; the fish, in butter and white wine was delicious, but Quentin didn't notice. He was struggling with the realisation that Stevie meant a lot more to him than he had thought.

They finished their meal. Quentin followed Stevie up the wide staircase. She wiggled; he tried to slap her bottom. She ran up the last few steps and they arrived at their room breathless, slamming the door behind them.

"What are you wearing under that dress?"

Quentin tried to kiss her but she pushed him away and with one movement swept the dress over her head and threw it onto the floor. She was completely naked. They fell on bed in a tangle of limbs, lips pressed together. Arranging and re-arranging themselves until they were panting for breath. Quentin struggled to get out of his clothes.

Stevie stopped him:

"That's not very romantic. You should lie still and let me slowly undress you."

Quentin tried to obey but couldn't help laughing.

"Quentin. Keep still and say the words."

He opened his eyes and wiped away a tear.

"What words?"

He tried to force her onto her back but she wriggled away.

"Say the words, Quentin."

He blinked, then what she was asking dawned on him. He reached out to her. "I love you so much, Stevie."

She pushed him over and they made love rolling over

and over until they fell off the bed and had to start all over again.

-§-

They were sitting up in bed with the breakfast tray across their knees. Stevie wiped her mouth on the back of her hand and smiled.

"Do you? Quentin, do you really?"

She was remembering what he said to her last night, in the throes of passion. She seemed to glow, like a well fed panther.

"Yes. The answer is yes, I do."

"What next, I wonder?"

It wasn't a question that needed an answer. She lay back on the pillows and shut her eyes, a smile hovered over her face; she drifted off.

Quentin went for a run along the front, past Humanity struggling out of the hedge and as far as the harbour. When he got back Stevie was in the shower. He joined her.

"We better get going. We can't hide in Wales for ever."

"Do you think Dave will come looking for you?"

"He might but that's not the point. I'm not afraid of him. He would never hurt me."

"You'll go back to Oxford to finish your degree then?"

"Of course, anything else is out of the question."

-§-

"Do you want to drive?"

Stevie laughed. "No Quentin. If it was a car I'd say yes but I've never owned a motorbike; I'd be sure to kill us both. As far as I'm concerned you're a safe pair of hands."

They set off down the winding Welsh roads, taking it easy, avoiding stray sheep and touring cyclists. The hills with their isolated farms tucked away under craggy cliffs gradually gave way to the rolling countryside of Shropshire. They stopped for a sandwich in Shrewsbury; shortly after that they were on the motorway and back in Oxford in time for tea. They left the Harley in Walton Street and Stevie showed Quentin up to her room in Somerville.

"Save water and shower with your steady?"

"There's nothing steady about either of us, Quentin. But yes and let's hurry up. I'm famished. Shall we try Browns?"

"Right."

The restaurant was not crowded but Quentin chose a table in a dim corner at the back. He sat facing the door.

"You look as though you're expecting someone," said Stevie.

"Well, it would be most unfortunate to meet Dave."

"Dave wouldn't make a scene here. And anyway I'm sure he's over me by now."

"You think so? He's the moved on already?"

"Yep, real men don't hang about."

"Even for you?"

"Especially for me, Quentin. I'm the one in a hurry around here."

"I've got a gig lined up at Dingwall's tomorrow. Do you want to join me?"

"I've got a load of work to do. Once finals are over I'll be free."

The waitress arrived and Stevie ordered rack of lamb.

"The same for me and a bottle of Malbec, please," said Quentin.

They ate in silence until Stevie wiped her mouth and smiled across the table.

"That's better."

"Pud?"

Stevie looked at the menu and then shook her head. They sat talking while they finished the bottle of wine.

"Can you put me up in Somerville?"

"No way. The walls are paper thin and the bed is much too narrow."

"I'll check us into the Randolph, then. Who do you want to be?"

"Stephany Rice-Davies."

"Rice-Davies isn't your real name is it?"

"Why not?"

"Your sister's called Mandy?"

"Perhaps."

"And perhaps not, Stevie. Please tell me your surname."

"Why? What does it matter?"

"It matters to me. I can't sleep with someone without knowing their name."

"You've done quite well so far."

"Thank you. I feel the time has come for formal introductions. My name is Quentin Griffiths, your humble servant."

Stevie bowed in acknowledgement.

"Stephanie Davies, pleased to meet you and to be served by you in the Randolph Hotel."

Quentin smiled.

"You're such a wit, Stevie."

"Just you wait, Mr Griffiths, just you wait."

-§-

Next day Quentin set off for London. Long distance high speed travel down open roads is what the Harley was built for and Quentin was enjoying himself. He hung onto the high handlebars and leant back as the bike carved a track through the traffic. Then at the first set of lights just as Quentin accelerated away, a taxi attempted a U-turn and they collided. Quentin's helmet smashed into the taxi's windscreen and he slid off the bonnet and into the road. Cars screeched to a halt. Drivers got out and started advising each other:

"Move him out of the road or he'll be run over."

"Don't, whatever you do, touch him; his neck may be broken."

"Are you a doctor?"

"Something like that."

"I'm a nurse, let me through."

Quentin lay in the road, stunned and unable to move. His leg seemed to be bent at an odd angle. There was no pain, but it was hard to make out what was happening. He pushed up his visor and undid the strap beneath his chin. The nurse got him to sit up and helped him remove his helmet.

"Keep still," she advised. "I think your femur is

fractured."

The Taxi driver sat in his cab in a state of shock. Police and an ambulance arrived and Quentin was moved onto a board, neck in a collar, head secured with straps. The ambulance moved off through the traffic, the blue light flashing. By the time they arrived in Accident and Emergency Quentin was cold and his leg was beginning to hurt something awful. He started to shiver. It seemed to take ages before the doctor arrived and when he did, he explained to the staff nurse that the patient was not to have any pain relief until the consultant had assessed him.

"He may have had a head injury. Don't let him dose off."

He said all this to the nurse without once looking at Quentin. Hours passed, but at last he was wheeled to theatres and the anaesthetist put him to sleep.

When he woke up, he was in a thirty bedded ward which seemed to be occupied half by boys who had come off their bikes and half by old men who had fallen and fractured their hip.

"They pinned your femur. You won't be here long."

The nurse, who looked even younger than Stevie, smiled as she shot Pethidine into his good leg. Quentin winced.

"Don't be such a baby. That didn't hurt."

"Thank you nurse. I could do with a lot more of that, please."

"No more for four hours at least. Just lie still and let the drug work. It'll be visiting time soon."

Nobody visited. Quentin wondered if anybody even knew he was in hospital. On day two he managed to ring his parents. He also left messages at Somerville for Stevie, just in case she was wondering where he was. Then on day four, just a day before he was to be discharged, they all turned up at once, including his sister.

"You can come home," said mother.

"That would be a squash. There's plenty of room at our house," said his sister.

At that moment Stevie entered the ward and the discussion had to pause while Quentin tried to introduce her.

"Are you his new girlfriend?" asked Sis who was always somewhat blunt.

"No," said Stevie.

"Just well acquainted then," said Dad.

Stevie smiled and nodded.

"I'll drive you back to Warkworth, when you're ready," she said.

"I didn't know you even had a car. Have you got a licence?" asked Quentin.

"Yes I have and yes I do, and I'm very happy to help, if that's what you want."

"He looks awfully pale," said Mum. "Perhaps a few days at home would be a good idea."

"Mum, he hasn't lived at home for twenty years. How could that possibly work?" asked Sis.

"Let bygones be bygones," said Dad.

"Stevie will look after me in Warkworth, won't you Stevie?"

"Sure."

"Well, we've got to catch the train home, or we'll have to wait until after the rush hour," said Mum.

The family left and Stevie sat on the end of the bed.

"I can't stay long in Warkworth."

"Perhaps you could just get me to the train then?" asked Quentin.

"No. I'll drive you if you don't mind sitting in a Mini for hours and hours."

"You've got a Mini now?"

"Yes. Mum gave it to me when she heard that I'd been riding up and down the country on your bike."

"It's her car then?"

"It's mine now. She's bought a new VW Golf."

"Posh!"

"Don't tease Quentin."

He laughed and reached forward for a kiss.

The next day, Stevie helped him put on his shoes and they took the lift down to the car park where the dark blue Mini was waiting. She was right. It was indeed a long and uncomfortable journey, despite frequent stops for Quentin to stretch his injured leg.

-§-

"You'll stay the night?"

"Am I invited?"

"Yes, of course."

Quentin limped across the one room that served as kitchen, dining room and living room and tried to kiss her but Stevie backed away.

"Ask nicely."

"Stevie, my love, stay for ever."

"OK but just one night is all I can spare, my old

crippled lover."

"I'm no cripple. At least not yet. Give a dog a chance."

"Can you limp as far as the pub? I'm not up to cooking and I don't trust you to serve up anything apart from beans and an omelette."

The Anchor was as smoky and smelly as ever but they did an excellent fish pie and a good variety of cask ales.

"I've got a job in New Zealand. I'll be flying out once finals are over."

"Really? When did this happen?"

Quentin was taken aback. He'd begun to think that he and Stevie were or might be, an item.

"While you were lying in hospital I was busy contacting yacht builders in Auckland."

"You'll be designing yachts?"

"And building them."

"Well done."

"As you know, it's something I've always wanted to do."

"I'll lend you my book on the Logan brothers."

"I had an interview over the phone. They were impressed when I told them I was doing a degree in engineering."

"As indeed they should be. I congratulate them on their excellent choice."

"They said lots of naval architects had applied, but they wanted me because I would bring a different set of skills to the project and not have any preconceived ideas."

"What is the project?"

"To build an ocean going yacht that will win a race

around the world: the Whitbread, you may have heard of it."

Quentin nodded but his thoughts were not on racing yachts, he was trying to take in the news that Stevie was about to leave for the other side of the world.

Later that night when they were in bed, Stevie hugged Quentin to her and whispered.

"Aren't you going to try to stop me?"

"No Stevie. I love you but I also want you to be free to follow your dream, to do your thing. If we meet up again in New Zealand or London, that'll be great. Your fate and mine; it's in the lap of the gods."

5

Stevie in New Zealand

Stevie could see dinghies sailing on Manakau Harbour as the flight from London made its final approach and touched down in Auckland. In the arrivals hall Bob was waiting for her; they walked out to the car park, found the pick-up and joined the rush hour traffic into the city.

"Does it always rain like this?" asked Stevie.

"In the spring it generally does. That's why we have rain forests."

Stevie was looking out of the window of the Toyota Hilux Surf.

"And what are those pine trees with the branches pointing up to the sky?"

"Norfolk Pines. They were imported from Norfolk Island; like a lot of the flora and fauna here, they are not native."

"And those trees?"

"We call them gum trees."

"Ah, yes, so do we," Stevie laughed.

The traffic was heavy and they made slow progress towards Bayswater Marina. The torrential rain slowly eased, leaving huge puddles in the road. They parked up and walked down the pontoon to where a Lidgard 38 was moored between piles. Stevie read the name painted on the side of the hull: Blue Grass. Bob pulled the yacht closer to the pontoon and Stevie heaved her kitbag into the cockpit. Bob opened up the main hatch and went below. Stevie followed him down the narrow steps into the saloon, noting the smell of damp wood mixed with a whiff of diesel.

"Wow, there's so much room," she remarked.

"You won't get lonely here. The liveaboards hold barbecues every Friday and there's plenty going on at Devonport Yacht Club. And in addition to all that you can have a good night out in Takapuna. But you will need a car. It's a long way to the shops and further to the club."

"I'll buy an old banger."

"I'll come with you. I know just where to go."

"Thanks, which bunk would you recommend?"

"Sleep in the forepeak, then you won't have to tidy away your stuff when guests come for supper. Mind your head on that beam though," Bob warned her.

Stevie ducked under a huge Kauri wood crossbeam and threw her bag onto the bunk.

Bob filled the kettle and put it on the hob. They sat round the varnished saloon table sipping their tea. Bob opened a packed of ginger biscuits.

"It's really kind of you to let me stay on your boat."

"No worries, eh. We'll take her out at the weekend."

Stevie sipped her tea.

"Where's the club?"

"In Devonport. I'll introduce you to my mates this evening. I've got some things to do now but I'll be back to pick you up about seven."

Bob went and Stevie busied herself unpacking her things and exploring the washrooms in the main car park. They were far more practical than the ones in Cowes; each cubicle was almost like the bathroom back home in her London flat. The pipped music played numbers by local bands. Not bad, thought, Stevie. I think I'm going to be happy here, and Bob seems really nice.

-§-

They parked outside the Devonport Yacht Club and walked through the yard, past boats that were undergoing maintenance and up the steps to the front door. Bob waved to his mates:

"This is Stevie, she's from Oxford. She's been recruited to help with the design and build of the new Steinlager."

"It's going to be a steep learning curve," said Stevie

"Bruce runs a tight ship, but he's fair. You'll learn a lot," said Dave.

"It's the practical side of things I need to understand."

"You'll get that in Auckland. We're nothing if not practical, eh Bob?" said Tom.

Bob nodded and went over to the bar to order for himself and Stevie.

"I'll get them in," said Stevie. "What will your friends have?"

Bob frowned, then smiled.

"They've got their drinks. We don't buy rounds here. It's everyman for himself but just this once I'm going to get you a drink."

Beers in hand they moved over to the buffet and then joined the others at a long table. The conversation was all about Peter Blake's new yacht. Bob had been on Lion when they came second in the Whitbread. They had only been back in New Zealand a few weeks and already the team was focused on the next event: the 1989 Whitbread.

-§-

The next day was Saturday and Bob appeared on the pontoon just as Stevie was coming back from the showers.

"I've brought some bacon and eggs. I thought we

could have breakfast once we were underway."

He handed her two bags of provisions. They cast off and headed out into the Hauraki Gulf. Stevie fried up eggs, bacon and tomatoes and flipped them onto buttered bread. She squashed the whole mess together and handed a plate up the companionway to Bob and went on deck clutching two cups of tea.

"We're just passing Bean Rock," said Bob pointing to a lighthouse perched on a spindly steel platform that looked like something out of the War of the Worlds.

"Good grub, by the way," he added.

They passed Rangitoto's perfectly symmetrical volcanic peak and left Motuihe to starboard. By lunchtime they were anchored up in Oneroa Bay, about a hundred yards from a long sandy beach.

"Fancy going ashore for a drink, Stevie?"

"Yes indeed! I'd like to see what the island's like."

The pulled the tender alongside and climbed in. Bob rowed and Stevie sat in the bows. One last heave of the oars the dinghy was on the sand. Stevie jumped ashore and pulled the dinghy up the beach. She tied it to a tree above the high-water mark.

"You'll need shoes," said Bob, looking at Stevie sandy feet.

"I thought everyone went barefoot in New Zealand," she said, retrieving her sandals from the bottom of the boat.

"Boys and girls often do, but in bars it's the rule that customers wear a shirt and shoes."

They climbed the zigzag path up the steep cliff and walked round the corner to Bays Edge. They sat on the decking, sharing a bottle of Villa Maria. They could see

Blue Grass bobbing at anchor far below.

"Do you live in Oxford?" asked Bob.

"Only during term time. My mother has a houseboat on Cheyne Reach."

"Where's that?"

"On the Thames in the centre of London."

"How convenient."

"It's alright in the summer. Where do you live Bob?"

"Devonport. I've got a bachelor pad not far from the club, but I spend a lot of time on the boat."

"Have I pushed you out?"

"Not at all. I'm only too happy to have a liveaboard looking after her. Especially as it's you."

Stevie wasn't sure what he meant by that, but she felt flattered.

They hired bicycles and rode around the island. It didn't take long. They returned the bikes and went into the art gallery next door.

"I wonder what they're showing," said Stevie.

Black and white pictures were on display, mostly nudes.

"The female form divine," said Bob.

"In such tasteful poses," Stevie laughed

Back on Blue Grass supper was very simple. Stevie heated up some meat balls in tomato sauce that Bob had bought in the New World supermarket that morning. They moved on to apple and cheese and washed the meal down with a bottle of Oyster Bay. Stevie had laid in a whole case.

"I had no idea wine would be so expensive here, it's

cheaper at home," she said. "After all, sauvignon blanc comes from vineyards in South Island doesn't it?"

"It does. The government heavily subsidises exports to make them competitive abroad but doesn't need to do that in the shops here."

"So that's why you bought Fosters this morning."

"Yes. I can't afford wine and I don't like Steinlager!"

"Why?"

"It's too sweet for my taste."

Stevie went to sleep in the forepeak and Bob took the quarter berth. She was woken at 2am by a change in the motion of the boat. The wind had swung round to the northeast and they were now on a lee shore. She pulled on her shorts and a sweater and went into the saloon. Bob was emerging from his bunk.

"We'll up anchor and move round to Owhanake Bay, it'll be sheltered there. We can't risk dragging the anchor and finishing up on the beach."

Bob started the engine and Stevie used the electric windlass to raise the anchor.

"This is so easy, on Dad's old gaffer it's all done by hand: brawn and brute force."

"He must be tough your old man. It's not light work sailing a gaffer."

"He is," she replied.

Blue Grass bashed her way through the chop, out of the bay into the open sea. Stevie hung onto the wheel. They turned down wind towards the shelter of Owhanake Bay and the yacht's motion settled. It was flat calm in the bay; the only noise came from the wind and the waves at the entrance to the deep inlet.

-§-

"Bye Stevie, thanks for a great week end."

"Thank *you* Bob. It was all down to you, obviously!"

"I'll come by tomorrow afternoon and take you to choose a car in Takapuna."

"I'll look forward to it. Bye Bob."

He's really nice she thought and quite good looking, different from Quentin, younger and less complicated. She heaved a sigh, Quentin was half a world away.

-§-

They were through the town and on the road to the Bays before Stevie even noticed the place.

"Was that Takapuna?"

"Yes, it was. We bypassed main street but we'll go back that way."

"I thought you said: one could have a good night out in Takapuna."

"And so you can if you have mates!"

They drove into the parking lot of a second hand car dealer. Stevie chose an old, rather battered Honda Civic; there weren't too many miles on the clock and she liked the royal blue paintwork, but the smell of the air freshener was overpowering. I'll soon sort that out, she thought. Bob drove on ahead and parked behind the shopping mall in Takapuna.

"What'll you have, Stevie?"

"It looks like everyone is drinking Guinness, but I'd

prefer wine, if that's OK."

"It's the Irish pub, if you were wondering, but I dare say they do Oyster Bay."

"Thank you Bob. I guess Van Morrison on the jukebox does rather give it away."

Bob ordered the drinks and then snapper and kumara chips. They moved over to a table at the back of the place.

"Do you like kumara? Stevie."

"The chips, you mean? They nice. I don't think we have them in England, at least not where I live."

Bob smiled.

"The October Race will get underway in a few weeks."

"What's that?"

"It's New Zealand's equivalent of your Round the Island Race."

"That sounds exciting."

"Yes. There are not so many boats involved as there are in the Round the Island Race but the sight of the fleet going out past North Head is impressive."

"So where does it start and finish?"

"The start is on the Squadron line and the finish is off the Duke of Marlborough Hotel in Russell."

"Forgive me Bob, but where is Russell?"

"Bay of Islands, about 125miles north of Auckland. It takes a good 24 hours to get there for the average family cruiser, allowing for wind and weather."

"I'm up for that. Are you going to enter Blue Grass?

"Of course. She's taken part every year except last year when I was doing the Whitbread."

"Great. What do we need to do to get the boat ready?"

"We'll take some weight off the boat nearer the time, but there's nothing to do right now."

They left the pub and Stevie drove back to Bayswater marina while Bob went back to his bachelor pad in Devonport.

-§-

The day of the race Stevie was up early. She had already taken the spare anchor and chain and deposited it in Bob's locker back at the club. It had been a major operation. She discovered that having pulled the chain out of its locker hand over hand into a huge basket on a trolley, she was not strong enough to lift it into the car. So she had to heave it fathom by fathom into the boot and then repeat the process all over again when she got to Bob's locker. Drink and then shower, or shower and then drink? she wondered and then, what if I meet Bob when I'm all sweaty like this? She decided to shower first and then went and sat at the bar and ordered a Steinie. She took a sip just as Bob sat down beside her.

"What'll you have?" she asked.

"I'll buy my own, thanks, Stevie. As I said we don't buy rounds in New Zealand."

"I feel I owe you."

"You don't owe me a thing. Let's eat here and then go back to Blue Grass. Mind if I sleep on board tonight? It'll be an early start tomorrow, eh."

"Of course. She's still your boat," she laughed.

-§-

The next day the whole fleet, nearly two hundred boats, were milling about in the region of the Harbour Bridge. The breeze was coming from the south west.

"Fancy a spinnaker start?" Bob asked.

"Do we have any choice?" Stevie frowned.

"I'd run down the line on starboard, bear away as the gun goes, and then hoist," said Tom.

"You could get into all sorts of trouble trying to time a spinnaker run with all these boats around you. I agree with Tom," said John.

"Safe but not fast," said Bob. "We'll have to play catch up with those that time it right. Still, we'll be well ahead of those that are early and have to go back."

"And windward boat keeps clear, which will be to our advantage," said Jake.

"I agree," said Dave.

"Decision by committee," said Bob. "I'll go with the majority."

Stevie felt the excitement rising as Bob manoeuvred Blue Grass towards the pin end of the Squadron Line. She and Tom were on the foredeck ready to hoist the spinnaker as soon as the order came. They were lying down to allow Bob a clear view.

"Starboard!" Bob and the others in the cockpit were yelling at a boat that was bearing down on them on port gybe, obviously hoping to get round North Head without having the trouble of gybing with boats all around them. They swerved out of the way and in doing so crash gybed.

"Their cunning plans went all awry," laughed Bob.

His glee was short lived as a larger yacht came up under their lee and started to shout: "Up you go!"

forcing them away from the line and stopping them from diving down and hoisting as the gun went. It was only a matter of seconds before the yacht bore away and hoisted but that was enough to leave them trailing in the wake of the bigger boat. Tom and Stevie raised the spinnaker pole into position.

"Go for it," yelled Bob to the two on the foredeck. Stevie freed the spinnaker from its bag and went to help Tom sweat the halyard.

"Made!" yelled Tom.

Blue Grass surged forwards as Jake sheeted in the huge red sail. But they were on starboard and to get round North Head they needed to gybe onto port tack.

"More excitement," said Tom as he and Stevie got ready to reposition the pole. "Not an easy task in a fresh breeze," he added.

"And we'll need to keep clear of those still on starboard," said Stevie.

"Indeed," said Tom as the crew in the cockpit started to play with sheets and guys, keeping the spinnaker flying as Bob slowly changed course, the main sheeted in. The crowds on North Head were cheering and waving as the fleet set a course to clear the Whangaparaoa peninsula. Bob sorted out the night watches. As the only female, Stevie was expected to cook as well as help on the foredeck, but that did not get her out of doing her night watches.

"It's the same the world over on racing yachts," said Bob.

"I think it will be a bit different on Maiden," she replied.

"They'll be too busy cooking and sewing to do any

sailing I should think."

"Bob! I'm shocked at you. Tracy Edwards and her crew are serious contenders. I'll bet you they'll be in the chocolates."

"OK. How much?"

"Dinner at the Regatta Bar!"

"You're on!"

The sun was setting over North Island as they crossed Bream Bay on a board reach, passing inside the Hen and Chicken Islands. The smell of Manuka flowers came on the breeze.

"That's the smell of New Zealand, Stevie. It tells the sailor he is home from the sea, or nearly," said Tom.

Bob had divided the crew into two watches; two hours on and two hours off. He handed over to Tom at midnight.

Stevie spent her watch sitting on the rail with John. She went below at midnight and fell into her bunk. The next thing she knew Bob was shaking her shoulder.

"Wakey, wakey."

"What time is it," she screwed up her eyes, trying to focus.

"2am. It's our watch."

She pulled on a jumper and struggled into her salopettes and sea boots. Bob took the wheel from Jake. Stevie and John sat on the deck with their legs hanging over the side and their heads under the guard wires.

"This isn't very comfortable," said Stevie.

"I'll get you a cockpit cushion," said John and returned with two. "It's worth sitting on the rail, even though it is a pain," he said. "It keeps the boat more upright and that's faster."

The dawn brought a flush of colour to the sky and soon the waves were a shimmering mass of reds and gold. A sparkling morning was taking shape.

"See those rocks up ahead?" he asked.

"Yes."

"They mark the entrance to the Bay of Islands, Russel is only a few miles further on."

Sensing that the race was coming to a climax the rest of the crew appeared on deck.

"Where are all the boats?" asked Tom.

There were no other yachts in sight.

"They've finished already," said Bob.

"They're miles behind," said Jake.

And indeed two yachts could be seen over by the mainland shore, well astern of Blue Grass.

"What's that passing the Hole in the Rock now?" asked David.

Bob got the binoculars. "It's one of the bigger boats," he said. "We might be doing quite well."

As the sun rose they drew slowly closer to the towering rocks, named after the arch that formed the hole. It was a beat to the finish, but by midday they crossed the line to a gun from the committee boat.

Stevie helped Tom get the tender out of the cockpit locker and inflated it. Then, dangerously over loaded, they went ashore to the Duke of Marlborough hotel.

"I've booked myself into a room for the night." said Bob, "but you're all welcome to use the shower."

"Ladies first," said Tom. "While you're showering we'll get some beers. There is a buffet laid out in the conservatory."

"Excellent," replied Stevie. "I won't be long."

"We'll be outside on the terrace," said Tom.

Stevie wrapped herself in a large fluffy white towel and used the smaller one to dry her hair. Goodness I do feel tired, she thought, I'll just lie down on the bed for a minute. She grabbed a dressing gown from the back of the bathroom door.

"Stevie, wake up you're missing all the fun."

Bob was leaning over her, shaking her by the shoulder. The dressing gown fell open and she pulled it back into place. She heard Bob take a deep breath as he slipped his hand under the robe and bent down to kiss her. She gasped, surprised, then she shut her eyes and pulled him down and returned his kisses. He pulled away and slid down the bed so that he could kiss her nipples.

"Go on, Bob" she said, "please don't stop."

Someone was banging on the door.

"When are you coming down?" Tom called.

"They're ready to clear away the buffet and you'll miss it if you don't come now," Jake added.

"Sorry, I fell asleep!" Bob called back. "I'll be with you in a minute."

"Where's Stevie?" asked the first voice.

"Isn't she with you?" said Bob.

"No," Tom replied.

Stevie went to hide in the bathroom as Bob pulled on his clothes and opened the door.

"She's probably exploring Russell," he said.

Stevie could hear them walking away down the corridor.

"I thought Stevie was with you, eh?" It was Jake this time. The remark was followed by sniggering. Oh dear, she thought, how am I ever going to live this down? Then: do I even care, I've fancied Bob from the moment we first met and now I know he fancies me! She dressed and hurried downstairs, went outside into the road and then came back by way of the veranda and so into the conservatory where the buffet had been laid out. It was nearly empty but the staff let Stevie and Bob load up their plates with what was left. They went over to a table overlooking the water.

"Wow, this is good grub. We should have got here earlier."

"We would have, Stevie, it you hadn't delayed us," Bob replied.

"Me? I think it was you!"

They finished up and went to join the rest of the crew in the bar. Tom and Jake were engrossed in a game of billiards, while the other two watched.

"When's the prize giving?" asked Tom.

"It'll start when the last boat gets in, so the rest of you have time for a shower," said Bob.

"Thanks, skipper," said Jake and handed his cue to John.

The prize giving started at 10pm.

Blue Grass was first in class. The whole crew went up to receive the cup and huddled around the skipper who held it aloft for photographs.

"Where are you sleeping tonight?" asked Tom.

"On board, of course," replied Stevie.

He put his head close to her ear, "Not with Bob in the hotel, then?"

"No Tom. We are not an item,"

"Really or do you mean you're just not quite sure he's what you want?"

"I like Bob, but I don't have that long in New Zealand. When Steinlager II is finished and my visa runs out, I'll have to go home."

"So, make hay while the sun shines, as we say in New Zealand."

Stevie laughed. I am going to have a fling with Bob, she thought. It'll be exciting and if I keep my head there's no reason for anyone to get hurt. He's a great guy, so kind and gentle, that's when he's not being the uncompromising skipper of a racing yacht, urging Blue Grass and her crew on to victory, and I don't think he can be that much older than me.

They finished their drinks and all except Bob piled into the tender and paddled back to Blue Grass. Stevie slept in her usual bunk in the forepeak. She had to share with Tom and even then it was a squash for the other three who had to choose between the double made by dropping the saloon table and the quarter berth. Jake decided to sleep in the cockpit.

"I think Bob was hoping for some company," said Tom.

"Oh?" Stevie yawned.

"Why else would he book a room?"

"Don't some skippers always sleep ashore after a race?"

"Maybe but not Bob."

"Well, he never asked me, so I can't comment."

And with that she fell asleep.

-§-

Stevie cooked breakfast for the boys: eggs, bacon, tomatoes and beans all fried up in the largest pan she could find. Bob appeared in the club launch just as they were finishing.

"I saw the Blue Peter flying and thought I better join you."

Stevie joined Tom on the foredeck and helped him untangle the mooring lines.

"All gone!" he shouted.

Bob eased the throttle forwards and Blue Grass headed out into the bay. Their course ran between huge rocks, then turned abruptly to starboard to avoid a shallow patch before approaching the Hole in the Rock. Bob swung the bows up into the wind and Tom and Stevie sweated the halyard as the main rose into the air and the crew in the cockpit winched away in a sudden frenzy of activity. They swung round, left the famous rock to starboard and set a course for home. Tom and Stevie settled themselves down on the foredeck, backs against the fore cabin roof.

"So why didn't you spend the night with Bob?"

"He's not my boyfriend. I only went to his room to use the shower."

"And then what happened?"

"Nothing. I lay down on the bed for a minute and fell asleep; I didn't mean to."

"And you were awoken by a kiss, like the Sleeping Beauty."

Stevie giggled, remembering how she was roused by Bob's fingers exploring her breast.

"No, nothing like that," she lied. "And anyway why are you so interested? It's nothing to do with you."

She got to her feet and made her way back to the cockpit holding onto the rail on the coachroof to avoid being thrown overboard as Blue Grass rolled. I hope Tom doesn't fancy me, she thought. I hope he doesn't think I'm one of those promiscuous English girls.

Blue Grass was running before the wind, surfing down the waves.

"Ten knots!" Bob pointed at the log. "Jake you take over, see if you can get any more out of the old girl."

Jake took the wheel. "Coming up," he called. "Sheet in a fraction."

The slight change of course was just enough to start the boat surfing down the next wave. They all watched the log as it climbed past ten knots and hovered at eleven. There was a cheer and John took over but he couldn't match Jake's effort. Stevie passed: "It's too much for me," she said. "The wind's got up and I'd hate to broach in these seas."

Bob took over the helm again and they surged onwards at a steady seven knots according to the GPS. "Tide must be against us," he said. "But it'll turn in three hours and we'll be home before midnight."

"I think I'll go below," said Stevie.

"Take a stretch off the land," said Bob and laughed.

"You like those old nautical expressions, don't you?" said Tom. "I think I'll do the same," and he followed Stevie down the companionway.

Stevie was already lying on her bunk when Tom came into the forepeak and got onto his, opposite her. Stevie turned her back on him and pretended she was already asleep. The next thing she knew, he had wriggled his hand under her T-shirt and was tickling her spine.

"Get off," she said rolling onto her back.

He slid his hand onto her middle. "Come on, don't pretend you're shy."

He tried to slip his fingers under her bra. She jumped off the bunk and whipped her knife out from under her pillow.

"Ha, ha, Tom. I forgot to tell you I always sleep with a knife under my pillow."

She waved it under his nose, then with a laugh she ducked under the crossbeam and went back on deck.

There was a screech and a loud curse. The noise came from Tom who had forgotten the solid kauri wood beam. Stevie crouched down and peered into the gloom of the cabin. He was sitting at the saloon table clutching his head and trying to staunch the flow of blood. She straightened up. "Somebody better go and help him," she said. "Looks like he nearly knocked himself out on that beam."

Bob handed her the wheel. "Keep on 180 degrees and mind the gybe," he said and went below.

"Don't you want to steer, Jake?" she asked.

"No it's your turn, but I'll warn you if I think we're about to gybe," he smiled.

"Why was Tom in such a hurry to leave the forepeak?" asked David.

"I threatened him with my knife, the one I keep under my pillow," said Stevie with a laugh.

She could see that none of the men in the cockpit believed her. They laughed too.

"If it was my boat I'd take a chainsaw to that beam," said John. "The number of times I've nearly brained myself leaving the heads."

By the time they reached Auckland harbour, the moon was high in the sky. Bob pointed out the Southern Cross to Stevie. They dropped sails as they passed the Devonport Yacht Club. The boom cover was put on and the fenders made ready as Bob eased Blue Grass into her berth.

"Well done old girl," he said patting the side deck. "And well done you too." He looked at Stevie and smiled. The others grabbed their bags and headed off to the car park. Stevie and Bob went below and arranged the double bed.

"Did Tom try it on?" asked Bob.

"Sort of," she answered, "but I explained to him that I'm not that sort of girl and I think he got the message."

Bob laughed. "Seems you're well able to look after yourself. Do you want anything before we turn in?"

Stevie shook her head and went to change in the forepeak, she stood looking at her bunk and listening to Bob cleaning his teeth in the galley sink. When she heard him settling down in the saloon she made up her mind and ducking under the beam slid into the bed beside him. He didn't seem surprised. Their love making was brief and so gentle that Stevie thought Bob might fall asleep before she was ready. He didn't. She gasped and held on tight.

"You're amazing," she told him and she meant it; she knew then that he would never let her down.

6

My Love, My Love

"Hi, Martin, how was your day?"

"Fine Denise, just fine. Did you get all your lines off by heart?"

She'd been in the University library studying the play we were to put on at the end of the year in the Minerva Theatre.

"And you?" she asked.

"Oh I'm not nearly there yet but because my part is so short they had me painting scenery today. How are you getting on with Romeo?

"He is such a pain in the arse. The next time he comes onto me I'll fix him."

"What do you mean, fix him? Don't do him in, we can't put on Romeo and Juliet without Romeo," I laughed.

"Why don't you play Romeo?"

"I wasn't asked and I'm not nearly handsome enough and I prefer Benvolio."

"You're too modest. You're not bad looking as blokes go and you are a far better actor."

"Now you seek to flatter, fair damsel, and besides as Benvolio I don't have so many lines to learn and I can sneak off to the pub once the fight scene is over."

"You're basically a lazy toad."

"It suits me being a lazy toad, there is always a chance a princess will give me a kiss."

"Lick."

"Lick?"

"Yes Martin, princesses lick toads because they give off a substance very like LSD."

"But quite poisonous, I'm told. So a light brush of the lips, a brief kiss but no licking, please."

Denise laughed and started looking through the kitchen cupboards for something to eat.

"Toad, did you do any shopping?" she asked.

"No, I didn't. I thought I would use up the rest of the bacon with a tin of beans. I wasn't expecting company."

"What will the others have when they get in?"

"It's Friday so Celia usually gets a pizza on her way home and Simon may bring something from the deli."

Denise had recently joined the three of us in a rented house in North Chichester, within walking distance of the University. I generally kept to myself and left the lovers to their own domestic arrangements. Denise had returned after the short Easter holidays to find her landlord had thrown her out.

"It wasn't my fault," she told me while we were having a break from rehearsals. "The two final year students had gone off leaving the place in a shocking state. They didn't care because they were not planning on coming back this term."

I didn't know Denise well but I already liked her a lot and I immediately offered her a place in the house I shared with Celia and Simon. It helped with the rent. The down side was that I had to move out of my room and sleep in the sitting room so that Denise could have the main bedroom with the en-suit.

"I'll treat you Denise," I said. "The pub at the end of the road does reasonable grub."

"You don't need to treat me. I don't mind eating out

seeing as it's the week-end."

We walked down to the Bell. I ordered pints while Denise looked at the menu.

"I'll have fish and chips," she smiled at me as I put a pint of Young's Original on the table in front of her.

I went back to the bar, made our order and picked up a wooden spoon with a number on it. I sat down opposite Denise and we started comparing notes, where home was and things like that. It turned out she came from Norfolk and her family owned one of those Norfolk Broad sailing boats.

"We ought to go sailing in Chichester Harbour," I suggested.

"Do you have a boat?"

"Indeed I do, or at least the use of one. The family have an Itchen Ferry on a swinging mooring off Westlands Farm."

"Itchen Ferry?"

"One hundred year old gaff cutter."

"Ah, wooden, slow smelly and leaky. Does she have cotton sails?"

"No Denise, we have upgraded to Dacron and even installed a 30hp Yanmar engine."

"That doesn't sound so bad. Dad absolutely refuses to have anything to do with engines in sailing boats."

"What do you do when the wind drops?" I asked.

"Apply the sweeps," said Denise and laughed.

The next week-end we cycled down to Westlands and rowed out to Kitty. I held the tender steady as Denise climbed into the cockpit and hauled our bags and provisions after her.

"You'll sleep in the forepeak," I told her. "The door has a lock on it and you have the heads and a basin all to yourself."

"Where'll you sleep then?" she asked.

"In the saloon. I just ask that you don't sit on my bunk in wet oilies."

Leaving Denise at the helm I went onto the foredeck and cast off, then stood by the mast.

"Bring her up into the wind and I'll hoist the main."

"Coming up now," she answered.

The varnished gaff rose slowly up the mast and once the peak halyard was tensioned the white sail set without a wrinkle.

"We'll have to motor-sail until we're over the bar," I said.

The wind was southwest.

"With the incoming tide against us we don't have much choice," Denise agreed.

Once out at sea we cut the engine and set a course for Bembridge; the wind was on the beam. Denise proved to be an excellent helm so all I had to do was set the yankee and staysail.

"Any chance of coffee?" Denise asked; she was enjoying herself.

"Coming up," I answered and went below to put the kettle on the gas. While I waited for it to boil, I stowed away the stores, putting the biscuits and chocolate into a large plastic box to keep on deck.

"You're so well organised," Denise remarked as I emerged from the companionway. "Here, take the helm."

She studied the chart plotter and sipped her coffee while I enjoyed the feel of the yacht responding to the wind and the waves.

"The approach to the Harbour can be tricky. Don't miss out any of the channel markers." Denise concluded.

"We'll get there just after high water, so we should be able to clear the bar," I answered.

"It won't do to go aground on a falling tide," she observed.

I called up the Harbour Master and was allocated a berth on the north side of the pontoon. We made it safely up the winding waterway to the harbour entrance and swung into our berth. The owners of a larger yacht and a motor boat hurried to fend us off and take our lines as we slipped into the narrow space between them.

"It's not really a marina as such," I explained. "Just one long pontoon but there are showers."

"Sounds like luxury."

We went ashore and after a brief stop at the office, walked along the Duver. It was early evening and the falling tide was exposing a long sandy beach. Denise was carrying a bag of swimming things.

"I'm going to strip off; avert your eyes," she announced and without waiting for me to reply pulled her t-shirt over her head and slipped out of her shorts.

"You were wearing your bathers all time."

"Sorry to disappoint you," she laughed.

I sat on the wall as she ran down the beach and plunged into the sea. She was such a confidant swimmer, and I am anything but, so I stayed put, sitting on the wall that divided the sand from the path, content just to watch her as she duck dived and floated on her back.

"Come in," she called.

"I can't swim," I called back.

Denise came galloping back up the beach and grabbed me. I couldn't resist and followed her into the water, leaving my shirt and shorts on the sand. Denise swam out and treading water watched me. I caught up with her and she dived again coming up underneath me and flipping me over. I surfaced coughing.

"You're like an Orca, attacking a seal," I spluttered.

We made it back to the shore, Denise pretending to shepherd me along like a lifeguard in a soap opera. Back on the sand she started performing handstands and turning cartwheels.

"Where's all this energy come from, Denise?"

"I'm just expressing how happy I feel," she replied.

"Are you always this jolly?"

"Yes," she said and turned another cartwheel. "Ouch, I've twisted my ankle," she cried. "Carry me up the beech, Martin."

She was limping but she didn't want me to examine her ankle. She just jumped onto me for a piggyback. The sprained ankle was forgotten once we were dressed again and on our way to the pub.

Back on Kitty, Denise opened a bottle of wine and we sat side by side on my berth in the saloon, taking it in turns to play a favourite song on the Bluetooth speaker. She was leaning against me and after a while we found ourselves horizontal, comfortably entwined. Kisses, gentle and experimental at first, became more urgent. I slipped my hand under her shirt, she had removed her wet swim things before we went into the pub.

"No underwear?" I whispered.

Denise didn't answer at once but undid my shorts.

"Speak for yourself," she giggled.

"Are you safe?" I asked.

Her eyes were shut. She pulled me down. "Yes, yes I am."

-§-

That was the beginning of a wonderful summer of parties and barbecues; long days cycling to the beach and back, sailing with friends in Chichester Harbour. Simon had a day-sailor moored at Dell Quay, which was more practical for short trips than Kitty. We ran aground, more than once, and each time it was Denise who jumped over the side and pushed us off. She was that sort of girl.

The play was coming on well too. Denise had finally managed to persuade Romeo that she was not going to be his girlfriend.

"I ate a whole clove of garlic and burped it up in his face in the middle of our love scene. That fixed him!" she laughed.

"I'm surprised he gave up so easily."

I was sitting beside her with my hand on her thigh; she slipped me one of her sideways looks and smiled.

"He has a very weak stomach," she said.

The four of us, Simon and Celia, myself and Denise were sitting at a table outside the pub. The sun was setting behind the trees but still able to send a shining path of golden light towards us across the water. Birds were heading home to roost. It had been a glorious, long, hot day. We had started early to catch the tide down to East Head and spent the day sun-bathing and swimming. Celia had made the picnic, but that seemed a long time ago now.

"Are we going to eat here or not?" Celia tried to bring us back to the present urgent business.

"Of course lovely. I'll get a menu."

Simon went off to the bar. Celia lent over the table and fixed Denise with her green eye. She had an alternating squint. One eye was green and the other was blue. If she fixed you with her green eye you knew she was going to say something serious.

"When are you two going to move into the bedroom? Simon and I want the sitting room back."

"So you can watch tele?" I asked.

"Partly and partly because we like to have somewhere to sit with friends when they come round for a drink"

"I'm already sleeping in the bedroom," Denise reminded her.

"I meant Martin, of course."

"I'll have to ask Denise," I said.

"Then ask her now."

"What now? In front of you and Simon?"

"What are we talking about?" asked Simon as he approached holding a menu.

"I'm going to ask Denise if…"

"She'll marry you!" Celia let out such a raucous laugh that people at tables around us turned to look at her.

This was my cue to go down on one knee.

"Denise, will you?"

"No! but you can move into my bedroom, if you promise not to snore."

We all burst out laughing and some strangers started clapping. Perhaps they thought that she had accepted me. Sadly she had not and never would.

As we got to know each other, our love-making became more imaginative. But after that first night we hardly discussed contraception. I left all that stuff to Denise. I heard her say to Celia that the pill made her put on weight. Barrier methods are unreliable and neither of us liked the interruption and the planning that that entailed. I suppose I thought that if she did get pregnant, then we would have to get married or something. The more I thought about it, the more wonderful idea of marrying Denise seemed. A dream that might come true. That is, until the day came when she announced that she had missed her period and the test was positive.

"Wow, darling, that's great!" I never normally called her darling.

She looked at me as though she knew something was up, her blue eyes swivelling sideways, "Oh," was all she said.

"We'll get married," I continued.

"Slow down, Martin. You haven't even asked me yet," she said.

"Will you marry me?" and then I added. "Please?"

There was a pause. Denise sat down and looked out of the bedroom window. In the garden the leaves were already golden and now the wind was tearing them off the trees. They were gathering in heaps around the neglected flower beds.

"No."

"No?"

"You heard me. Never."

"But…?"

"I've got things to do and my plans do not include you and a baby."

That took the wind out of my sails. I had not for a moment considered Denise's feelings. I looked down at the carpet and then up at the ceiling. Anywhere that would avoid her eyes. When I did dare to face her, she seemed to have shrunk into herself. She clasped her arms across her chest and started to rock backwards and forwards. Tears ran down her face and onto her summer dress. I moved around the bed and hugged her. For a long time we sat there. I was clinging to her; she was looking away.

She heaved a sigh. "I've made an appointment with the clinic."

"With the GP?"

"No. You can go straight to the clinic."

"We should talk this over before you do anything."

She turned on me, her face all screwed up. "Too late for talking. I've made up my mind. Now leave me alone."

I went down to the Bell and had a couple of pints. Although it was still early there were other students there that I knew and we got chatting. Somehow I didn't feel like getting plastered and after a while I just sat there listening to their conversation, not contributing much. They were discussing fuel injection.

-§-

Denise left the house very early the next morning so we didn't have a chance to have the important conversation

I had planned. When she came home there was nobody in the house. We were all busy at college. When I did get back I fiddled about in the kitchen making tea and toast. I thought I was all alone so I went up to our bedroom. That was when I heard a groan coming from the en-suit.

"Denise?"

There was another groan then silence. I called again and waited.

"Help…help…oh please… I need a doctor."

Then a thud.

"Denise! Are you alright?" I shouted.

Of course she was not alright. What an imbecile thing to ask but I was in a panic. My mind went completely blank. Then I made the first of several mistakes. I tried to get the door of the en-suit open. I tried to get to Denise to help her. The door was locked, but you can open a bathroom door from the outside by using a coin. My pockets were empty so I went down to the kitchen and took a knife from the drawer. But even with the lock open I couldn't get in. Denise had fallen across the door. I still did not call an ambulance. Instead I battered at the door until I had broken down a panel and could peer inside. Denise was unconscious curled up in a ball, still clutching her stomach. She was white. I mean colourless and there was blood everywhere: a huge amount of blood. I still could not get to her. At last I realised I had to dial 999.

Fire, Police and an ambulance arrived. But it was all so slow. I ran downstairs and let them in. They went straight to the bedroom but they could not get to Denise. The firemen smashed the frame of the door and pulled the whole thing into the room. Only then could they reach her and by then she had lost so much blood. There was no hope, I seemed to know that. But even so we all went along with the idea that she might be saved. She was put on a stretcher and awkwardly and slowly the paramedics carried her down to the ambulance. The siren and the blue light started and she was taken to Accident and Emergency. I followed on my bicycle. I sat in the waiting room for what seemed like an age and all the time I knew that Denise was dead.

The doctor came up to me as I sat there in that desolate room, my hands in my lap just staring into space. I was completely numb. He beckoned me to follow him and we went into a smaller, more private room. It looked like a room where staff might sit and share coffee. It was shabby but comfortable.

"I am so sorry," he began. "We did all we could but I'm afraid we were not able to save Denise."

He got her name right, and subconsciously I thanked him for that. It's not easy being a doctor in these circumstances.

"Can I see her?" I asked.

My voice was flat; I felt no emotion. Later I realised that I must have been in shock.

He nodded and led the way to the cubicle where they had attempted to resuscitate Denise. It was remarkably tidy. She was lying on her back in a clean white gown and her hands were folded across her chest. She might have been asleep except that she was so pale and her lips were so blue. I looked at her for a moment and then turned away. I think the nurse who stood beside her, sort of protecting her, expected me to kiss those cold blue lips but I didn't. I regret that now, but at the time I felt spent, washed out, unable to think or do anything.

"Thank you," I said and walked away.

The nurse hurried after me. There was a lot of information she had to impart. All I took in was that I had to attend the office next day to get the death certificate.

"That's if you are the next of kin," she added.

"No," I said "I'm not, but I will let her Mum know what has happened."

As I said that the flood gates opened and I started to cry, silently at first and then with great gulps of air and a horrible high pitched whine.

"Come and sit down," said the nurse. Her name was Cora. "It must be a terrible shock. Is there anyone at home to keep you company tonight?"

I shook my head. She led me back to the sitting room and made me a cup of tea. I sat there sipping it and wishing I could be on my own. At last she let me go and I bicycled home.

-§-

"Denise is dead," I had to say it out loud and even then I could not believe it. It sounded wrong, like I had got my lines all mixed up and said my final piece too soon. It was all so unreal. Then I said it again and I began to believe it. Beautiful Denise, she would never do all those things she had planned and I would never marry her.

-§-

I didn't know Denise's mother well. I'd seen her once or twice when she dropped things off for her daughter and once when we visited her family home in Bromley. I think she needed to get a pair of shoes or something. Mrs Walker had made me a cup of tea. I'd never met her father. My immediate thought was to leave it all to someone else. Perhaps the police had already sent an officer around to the house.

-§-

"Anyone home?"

Celia slammed the front door and barged into the kitchen, for such a small slight girl Celia certainly made a her presence felt. She habitually hailed you as if from the quarter deck of a ship in a storm. I think her father was a captain in the Royal Navy. It was a huge relief to see her.

"What's wrong? Your eyes are bright red; you haven't been crying have you?"

"Denise is dead."

Celia frowned as if not sure she had heard me correctly. She shook her head and went to put the kettle on. Then she turned back.

"Dead? Are you sure? What happened?"

I didn't answer immediately, I had to steady my breathing; it was an effort to think.

"She bled to death, in the bathroom, I was here."

"In the bathroom?"

"Well, no, in the en-suit. I couldn't get to her. She bled to death in front of my eyes."

"You saw her and did nothing?"

"No, no, it was not like that. She was stuck behind the door."

"Did the ambulance come?"

"Yes and the fire brigade and the police."

"So she died in hospital?"

"Yes and now I have to tell her mother."

Celia sat down suddenly, like a great weight was crushing her. She and Denise were, had been, great friends. She was leaning forwards, her head in her hands, as if trying to take it all in. Then she looked up at me.

"Why was she bleeding?"

"She was pregnant."

"And she had an abortion." Celia finished the sentence for me.

I could see the full horror of it all beginning to dawn on her. I got up and tried to put my arms around her but she slipped off her chair. When Simon came in he found us like that: clutching onto each other.

"What are you doing?" he sounded confused, almost angry as if he had caught us making love on the kitchen floor. At that we both lost all control and started sobbing. Eventually Simon managed to get the whole story. He didn't cry but I never saw him look more serious than he did that day.

"I'll phone her mother," I said.

It turned out that they had already heard, in fact the police woman was still in the house. Later I had to give a statement. And then there was the funeral to attend. I would not have gone but for Celia and Simon's encouragement.

-§-

"What does one wear to a funeral?" asked Celia.

"Black," I said while trying to tie my long black tie.

"No, something cheerful," said Simon. "We should be celebrating her life."

"That comes later," I said. "Just now we are burying her, putting her into the cold dark earth."

"I thought she was going to be cremated," said Celia.

"Buried or cremated, in the end it's all the same. We are going to say goodbye to her. Forever."

"Not necessarily," said Celia. "She may come back to haunt you."

"Do you believe in ghosts?" asked Simon.

"No," I said.

"Yes," said Celia.

"In that case," I said "You better wear something bright and cheerful to please her and make her feel happy. Then perhaps she won't come back to haunt us."

"YOU," said Celia. "She will come back to haunt you. You're the one she loved."

A lump rose in my throat. I thought I had got over the worst of the pain but even now, weeks on, I was still being caught out by a sudden rush of emotion that had me putting my face in my hands, tears running down between my fingers. Someone suggested Valium, but somehow I preferred the pain. In a way, I was already afraid that the day would come when I would forget her, find it hard to remember her face, her scent.

The funeral was held in a small country church near her home in Bromley. We didn't know the family or even her school mates, so we sat right at the back.

Mother, father and an older brother who I had never met, read eulogies which seemed false to me. I began to think that they didn't understand Denise at all. Then a school friend stood up at the lectern and read a poem about a ship disappearing over the horizon. It all seemed unreal. Later, I realised I had been only a small part of her life, just the last few months in fact: that hurt.

Afterwards people went back to the house for sandwiches and drinks. We didn't stay long. I had this awful feeling that in some way the family blamed me for her death, and I could see why. I wanted to explain that we had discussed marriage but she had rejected me, but I couldn't. It was too personal and anyway that seemed cheap, an easy way out. I didn't feel I could relate that last conversation we had had in our bedroom.

"I feel sick," I whispered to Celia.

"Let's get out of here," she said and signalled to Simon.

We didn't even stop to say goodbye to the parents. The way people were looking at Celia made me feel uncomfortable. She was wearing a red dress with ivy embroidered around the hem. It stopped above her knees and showed off her figure to advantage. It might have pleased Denise's ghost and even her brother, but I could tell that her mother and her father disapproved. The school friends were all wearing black.

-§-

Years later, I went back to Chichester. The Festival Theatre was putting on Romeo and Juliet and I was to play Benvolio. The wheel was coming full circle. At first I had not wanted to take the part, I was afraid of the memories that might come back to haunt me. But then I began thinking about Denise. "Go for it!" she would have said. I could hear her voice, feel her breath on the back of my neck. It all seemed so real that I turned around expecting to see her. I wanted to hold her so, so much. Then I knew I would be playing Benvolio again, whatever the cost.

We had finished for the day and I was changing back into my jeans when there was a knock on the dressing room door.

"Celia! Where have you sprung from?"

"I live in Chichester, as you would know if you had bothered to keep in touch, you old toad."

"Don't say toad. Say warhorse or something nice."

"Does toad upset you?"

"Yes. I don't suppose you knew but that is what Denise used to call me."

"Really? It suits you. Now more than ever; you're starting to get a bit jowly and mottled."

"I haven't removed all the makeup. It was the dress rehearsal to-day."

"I know. I popped in to wish you well; break a leg and all that."

"Aren't you coming to the first night?"

"No, it's sold out."

"I'll ask the director to squeeze you into his box."

"Box?"

"Well, that's what he calls it. It isn't a proper box as such, the theatre here being so modern and original and all but he does have seats tucked away at the back where he and his closest friends can congregate."

"What do you have to do to become his closest friend?"

"Don't ask Celia. It would make a young girl like you blush."

Celia changed the subject. "What are you doing this evening, Martin?"

"Heading over to the Bell. Come with me if you can spare the time."

We walked across the car park and crossed the road to the pub. It had been one of our favourite watering holes when we were students, but I hadn't been in for a while since most of my work was in London, or if I was lucky, abroad. Celia nodded to one or two regulars. It was as if she had never left Chichester. She sat down at a table and I went to the bar to get drinks.

"Where are you working now?" I asked her.

"Rolls Royce, same as ever, except that I'm not an apprentice now."

"Oh?"

"I did a spell abroad, at the Mercedes headquarters in Stuttgart, which was a bit of luck because after that RR were keen to have me back."

"I'm not surprised, but what do you do, exactly?"

"Head of development. It's all about electric engines now, and I just happen to know more about that than anyone else on the planet."

Dear Celia, she hadn't changed a bit, full of confidence and boundless energy. I remembered how she and her then boyfriend had supported me through the dreadful times after Denise died. She fixed me with her green eye.

"Why have you come back to Chichester?"

"Work."

"But you're well know now, almost famous. I guess there are better things you could be doing."

"You flatter me, almost." I laughed.

"But there's something else, I sense," she went on. The green eye fixed me while her weaker blue eye wandered off. Celia could be disconcerting at times.

"I've been thinking about Denise. It's like she's at my elbow, as I go through my day I talk to her, ask her things."

"Like what?"

"Anything, everything, just whatever is on my mind."

It was a relief to say the words. Denise's presence had become almost oppressive and it was reassuring to talk to someone who had known her well, even loved her. Celia and I had been close, not lovers as she had Simon, but all the same good friends. She looked thoughtful, slowly nodded her head and then put an arm around me and gave me a hug.

"She haunts you still."

"It's the smell of blood," I said. "It wakes me in the night and I hear her calling out. I can't get to her and then I wake up sweating and find my pillow wet with tears."

Celia got up and pulled me to my feet.

"Come on," she said "I've got some eggs and leftovers at home. I'll make you an omelette."

We got out into the fresh air and I took some deep breaths.

"What happened to Simon?" I asked. Since we hadn't mentioned him at all, I sensed that maybe they weren't an item any more.

"I don't know. He didn't get the job at RR he wanted and he sort of went downhill. I think he works for Birmingham council now. We've lost touch."

When we got to her house, just off North Street, I realised that she must live on her own. It was one of those small but perfect Georgian houses overlooking the Park. There was a coat-stand in the hall but no coats on it and no random shoes under it, no washing up in the sink and no-one calling out. "Is that you darling?"

"Do you prefer living on your own?" I asked.

"No," she answered, she looked away, tears in her eyes. "I had a girlfriend but we didn't get on and then I realised I prefer men, but all the nice blokes seem to be taken. I'm getting old, Martin."

"You and I, Celia, we are not old. We have our lives before us."

She put her arms around my neck and kissed me. It was as if she had wanted this moment for a long time. The omelette was forgotten.

THE END

Footnote.

The idea that Celia might have one green eye and one blue eye came from a painting by Tony Trowbridge (tonytrowbridge.com)

Jubilee

It's our jubilee too, not platinum but gold. The Queen is celebrating all those years on the throne, but we are celebrating our twenty five golden years. We met at Uni. She was my first love. My only love at a time when most of my friends seemed to flit from one girlfriend to the next. I was in awe. She told me later that she thought I was shy and needed bringing out.

"Bringing out?" I asked her when she was teasing me about our first date all those years ago. "What do you mean?"

"You were a country boy, new to London and girls. You didn't know a thing. I felt I had to teach you."

She turned up at my hall of residence wearing a huge blond Dolly Parton wig. I'm sure I was meant to laugh but I couldn't. I just stood in the door of my room and gaped. She took the wig off and her long dark hair fell around her shoulders.

"Let's go," she said.

"Go where?" I asked.

"The Black Cap."

We took a bus to Camden.

Annabel went straight up to the bar and ordered drinks.

"A glass of Hirondelle, please," she said to the barman and then swung around to me. Before I could say anything she had turned back to the bar and ordered a pint of London Pride.

We sat a corner table. A woman in a white, skin tight, sequined dress was being helped up onto the stage.

"This bloody frock is far too tight, no wondered she died a virgin!" I heard her say in a deep and husky voice. The outfit in question was tight from the high neck to the knees and then flared out and trailed along the floor. She looked like a film star.

"Marlene was no virgin," said the other and they laughed.

The band climbed onto the stage and the drummer settled himself down, the fiddler tuned up and the accordion played a few tentative notes. Marlene sat on a barrel. She started to sing:

Falling in love again
What am I to do?

"She's a man isn't she?" I whispered. Annabel's eyes seemed to pop out of her head and her mouth opened in a show of surprise that did not fool me.

"Have you never seen a drag queen?" she asked.

I went to the bar and ordered another round.

-§-

So began our life as students in London. Our favourite haunts come back to me: the Tate Gallery on a Sunday afternoon, the Vauxhall Bridge Tavern on a Friday night, the National Film Theatre and at the Royal Opera House. We watched Swan Lake from the gods, leaning over the balcony to get a glimpse of the dancers' heads. In the second year we moved into a basement flat in Earls Court. The place was damp; cups and plates piled up in the sink. It was a magical time. I passed finals and got a job in Brighton. Annabel was already working as an illustrator of children's books, so she was not tied to any particular place and moved with me. We rented a house in Kemp Town, not far from the Royal Sussex County Hospital. We had lodgers: a doctor and a nurse from the same unit where I worked. Sacha was my registrar.

"One day we will be rich and famous ENT surgeons," she said.

"Roll on the day, Sacha. I'm tired of being a dogsbody."

We were knocking off after a week-end on-call.

"I need to swim and lie in the sun," said Sacha. "Want to meet me by the Angel?"

"Right," I answered. "I'll bring Annabel along." Sacha didn't look too pleased.

When I got home I couldn't find Annabel. Later it turned out that she had gone up the Downs to sketch a woodland glade for a book she was illustrating. I got my swimming things and jogged along to the Angel. Sacha and her friend Annie were there, with other nurses I vaguely knew, all stretched out in the sun like so many seals but more curvaceous let me say, before they read this and come looking to kill me.

"Pass the sun tan cream," said Sacha.

Annie passed it to her and she threw it at me.

"Do the bits I can't reach."

I started on her shoulders and worked my way down her bare back to her bottom.

"Now do up my top. Leave my legs alone. I can do those myself."

I watched as she sat up and applied the lotion to her

legs. I could feel myself burning.

"I need to cool off," I said, heading for the sea.

Before I knew what had hit me Sacha was on my back and I was plunged head first into the waves. I struggled to my feet and swaying under her weight staggered towards the shingle. Although she was only a slight thing she managed to overbalance us. She pinned me down.

"Surrender?"

"Yes."

I was choking and gasping and laughing all at the same time. Sacha was delighted, her green eyes sparkled. We lay side by side listening to the long withdrawing roar of the waves dragging the shingle back into the sea. What next I wondered.

"Pub, grub, bed," she said as if reading my thoughts.

-§-

The 'affair Sacha,' as we later called it, put a strain on our relationship. But Annabel was a fighter and was not going to let Sacha have her way. As a result I gave up all idea of becoming an ENT surgeon and became a GP in Oxford. We married twenty five years ago and have been living in Meadow Cottage for at least twenty. Across the meadow is the River Cherwell. We can punt downstream to the Boathouse for a meal. We both play in a band. I have been known to sing *Falling in love again*. But in truth I have never not been in love with Annabel.

Spring

"Ring-a-ring-a-roses, a pocket full of posies" sang Abbi.
"Quiet, child," said her mother. "Your father hates that song."
They were sitting on the bench at the bottom of the garden, warmed by the early Spring sunshine, surrounded by yellow flowers and fresh green shoots.
"Why, mother?" asked Abbi.
"Dad and his brothers used to play down by the river. They had built a den of branches and leaves. One day some girls from the village discovered their hiding place. The girls started to sing that song. The three boys came out to see what was going on. The girls surrounded them and kept on chanting. They were holding hands and prancing round the boys. Ben was the smallest of the three and he started to cry. The girls whirled around them faster and faster, moving closer and closer to the river bank. The singing got louder and louder. The tallest girl, called Maureen, tripped and fell into the river. She was so strong she dragged all the others with her; she and your Dad swam to the bank. The others were swept away and drowned in the weir.
"What happened to Maureen?" asked Abbi.
Mother smiled, her eyes flashed.